THE DUKE AND THE DEBUTANTE

NICOLE BENNETT

CHAPTER ONE

NATHANIAL WARE, 7th Duke of Milton, eyed the ballroom before him with a wariness he hadn't felt in a long time. Barely two hours into his arrival and he'd already been introduced to a veritable host of blushing, wide-eyed debutantes eager to secure him for a set. As it was, none had achieved this lofty aim, though he knew it would only be a matter of time before he'd need to dance with *someone,* if only to settle his mother's increasingly obvious exasperation.

As if on cue, the duchess let out a huff of annoyance under her breath. "Really, Milton," she said with a tight smile as the most recent introduction went on her way. "When you said you were ready for the wife hunt, I expected you to put forth the tiniest shred of effort. How is anyone to know you are in the market for a bride if you refuse to speak to a single debutante for more than a string of sentences, mm?" Resplendent in a fashionable French ballgown and adorned in the

Ware Emeralds, the duchess was a sight to behold, her famed beauty not faded with age. Though she wore a frown, her blue eyes glittered with more mirth than irritation. "A part of me wonders if this sudden and recent admission of yours was merely a ploy to get me to attend the Season this year."

Nathan put a hand to his chest. "You shock me, madam. I am devoted to my duty to the bloodline, and I'll not have you question me with such silly accusations."

She raised a slender eyebrow in response. "Yes, and that was why you foisted funds for an entirely new wardrobe on me. Goodness, I haven't had so many new clothes since my come-out."

He could only smile and take a sip of tepid champagne in response. It had been almost ten years since his mother had ventured from the principal family seat, his boyhood memories of her as a social butterfly being just that, memories. Every day that went by seeing her doddering around the estate, the vibrant colors she once wore replaced with black, her wide smiles now ones of gentle melancholy, was like a punch to the gut. When he'd shown a tentative interest at the beginning of the month for a bride and she'd offered to accompany him to aid in his endeavor, he'd lept upon the chance to get his mother to London once more. And though his enthusiasm for the marriage mart had been just a tad exaggerated, the duchesses's blooming glow as she commanded every event they attended more than made up for the tedium.

"If you think I don't know your plots well, my dear boy, you are sadly mistaken," she said with a playful tap of her fan on his shoulder.

Nathanial pat her back with a chuckle. "Yes, I am more than aware of how shrewd you are. Though my happiness regarding the matter at hand might not be entirely honest, it is true that I am hoping for a wife soon."

"Hoping? Or resigned?"

"A bit of both, I think."

The duchess scoffed. "If you are serious, then you should stop making such a sour face any time the topic is brought up. And for goodness' sakes, dance. There must have been a dozen ladies introduced to you tonight. Has not one struck your fancy?"

"Dreadfully dull, the lot of them."

"Nathan!" she hissed, barely concealing a bubble of laughter with her fan.

"So you agree that this Season and the persons taking part within it have been lackluster."

"I will admit that, compared to a few years ago at least, these events have been..." The duchess tapped her chin. "What is a good way to describe it?"

"Boring?" he supplied.

"Must you be so blunt about things?"

"The blessings of a dukedom, I'm afraid."

She rolled her eyes. "Your father used to say the same thing."

A pang hit him at the thought of his sire, but Nathan concealed the pain with anther sip of his drink. That his mother could even speak of her husband so candidly without that empty look in her eyes was a great deal of progress that he would not discourage. "That he did."

"Oh, lovely," his mother deadpanned. "Lockhart is here and making a beeline for us."

Nathan perked up at the mention of his best friend and scanned the crowd in search of the man, soon spying him leisurely making his way over. Several women tittered as he passed, Lockhart occasionally stopping to chat with a blushing lady or two. While Nathan was a prime catch due to his title, Lockhart could command a ballroom through sheer seductive charm alone, and the man well knew it. A rather ludicrously handsome, infamous flirt known for his string of lovers, the baron was the prize of debutantes and bane of mamas alike.

"Milton! Lovely to find you here," Lockhart said. He turned to the duchess and kissed her proffered hand. "And you as well, Your Grace."

"And what brings you to such a mundane affair, Lord Lockhart?" she inquired without missing a beat. Out of all of his friends, Lockhart tended to irritate his mother the most, if affectionately so.

"Desperation, unfortunately," he replied. "The Season has been dreadfully dull, so much so that this staid ball is the most exciting event I've attended in weeks."

"Sadly, I fear you may be correct." She gave Nathan a knowing look. "I'll leave you men to it, for I know if one of your ragtag group is here, then the others are sure to follow."

"True indeed, Your Grace. Thurmont and Kirkwood are loitering about as we speak."

"Hiding, more than likely," Nathan replied with a snort into his glass. That the two were even here was surprising.

"And I am sure you will join them, considering the way tonight has gone," his mother replied, her tone lightly scolding. "I'm off to socialize, then. Behave yourself while I am gone."

"I will," he replied with no small amount of amusement. His mother well knew the sort of mischief that could arise when all of his friends were afoot. They weren't one of the most infamous sets in the Ton for no reason, after all.

"He won't get into any trouble with me around," Lockhart chimed in.

"Lying does not suit you, Lord Lockhart. I do recall that whenever there was mischief afoot at school with my son, you were almost always at the center of it. Alas, I fear Milton has about reached his limit for the evening, and the company of friends, questionable as they are, would do him well." The duchess gave Nathan one last pat on the arm. "I will leave you to your manly talk. Goodness knows I'll not want to hear what sort of adventures you lot have been up to."

They watched her disappear into the throng before Lockhart remarked, "You truly were serious when you informed me of the future bride hunt, I see."

"Part of it had more to do with cajoling my mother out of her seclusion, but yes, it is getting to be that time." Much as he dreaded the whole affair. If all had been right with the world, then the succession would have been entirely out of his purview. But nothing had been right for the past ten years.

Lockhart winced, his blue eyes crinkling in displeasure, as well he would. Nathan wasn't sure he knew anyone as averse to matrimony as the man before him. "Perish the thought," the baron said. "It is times like this that I am glad to have a younger brother who is devoted to the shackles of marriage and the gaggle of boys he seems determined to produce." He stiffened, looking at Nathan with obvious panic. "Oh, Christ. That was a thoughtless remark to make around you. Forgive me."

"It has been ten years," he replied, managing to keep his countenance even. "I can handle talk of siblings without crumpling into a heap." He loved his friends dearly, but their extra care around him whenever the topic came up was grating on occasion. While ten years ago the mere mention of Andrew might have sent him into a spiral, these days he only felt a dull throb of sadness at the memory of his older brother.

The guilt, however, was another thing entirely.

"I see your thoughts of matrimony haven't changed," Nathan remarked, hoping to steer the conversation towards lighter ground for both their sakes.

Lockhart grinned. "And never will. You are alone

in your efforts, I'm afraid, and will have to be content with the rest of us rooting for you from the sidelines, as good as that will do. I think you've picked just about the dullest year to embark on your quest."

Nathan sighed. "Believe me, I am well aware. At least your presence is giving me a break from these insipid introductions."

"My reputation does precede me." Lockhart smiled at a young lady and her mother as they passed, the older woman having to all but drag her moon-eyed daughter away from them. Nathan might be the catch of the season, but he doubted any mama was willing to risk exposure to Lockhart for a mere introduction.

"Things must be tedious indeed for you to be here. I think this is the first respectable entertainment I've seen you at all this spring. Kirkwood and Thurmont's attendance is also a mystery, though I haven't seen them all evening." He'd been so focused on shepherding his mother about and ensuring she was well that he'd thought little about the potential presence of the rest of their merry gang.

"That is why I've been looking for you, actually. Kirkwood finally got sick of his mother's pestering and decided to attend, dragging Thurmont along for emotional support. They're hiding in the garden at the moment and could use some company."

Nathan hesitated. "My mother..."

"Is fine." Lockhart pointed into the crowd. "She seems to be engrossed in conversation with Lady Drummel and having a grand time, as she should."

Nathan followed Lockhart's gesture and spied his mother talking animatedly with the viscountess, whom he could dimly recall being an old friend of hers. "I see."

"And her daughters are there as well. Goodness, Miss Caroline Hughs is just as striking as she was last year."

He assumed Lockhart was referring to the platinum blonde standing behind Lady Drummel. Indeed, the young woman was a sight to behold, as the rumors had suggested. Though this was his first time in polite society for quite a while, he was well aware of the debutante, famed for both her beauty and the peculiar fact that she somehow escaped her debut season last year without a betrothal. She seemed nice enough, the smile on her face as she surveyed the room sweet and uncontrived. Nathan was debating whether to put her on his tiny list of marriage candidates when she shifted, revealing another woman by her side. The facial features were similar enough to tell him that her companion must be the sister, though for the life of him he could not recall her name. A shame, really, for though she paled in comparison to her sibling, something about the lady drew his attention. There was a straight ease to her stature and an analytical glow in her brown eyes as she surveyed the crowd that told him she was smart as a whip. Her lips curved, as if on the cusp of uttering some witty rejoinder, and he caught himself leaning forward in anticipation despite his place on the other side of the ballroom. And then her gaze fell upon him, their eyes meeting in a clash of blue and chestnut. Nathan smiled his most charming grin and nodded. The woman's smile fell, of all things, and she titled her head, staring at him as if he were some bizarre animal she'd come across on a woodland stroll rather than the most eligible peer in England. Fascinating.

"What is her name?" he said, reluctantly tearing his gaze away from the riveting woman.

"Miss Caroline Hughs, as I stated a mere three seconds ago. Are you foxed already?"

"No, the other one."

Lockhart furrowed his brow. "The elder Miss Hughs? I'd be wary of her. She has quite the reputation."

"Oh?" To his disappointment, by the time he looked back, Miss Hughs had already turned away and was conversing with Miss Caroline.

"She had two failed seasons before Miss Caroline's come-out. After that, of course, she was entirely over-shadowed, almost to a pathetic degree. A perpetual wallflower, that one. I'd feel sorry for the woman if she wasn't so awful about it."

"Awful? How so?"

Lockhart sidled closer, speaking like a gossip mongering fishwife. "She has a tendency to be prickly towards gentlemen."

Nathan rose an eyebrow. "Prickly, or not willing to suffer fools?" He could imagine her setting down a frivolous fop with gusto. Most men disliked having their pride torn to shreds, even if warranted. As a young man, Nathan himself might have been counted amongst such a lot.

"Perhaps," Lockhart replied with a shrug. "But there are also rumors that she is rather bitter over her prettier sister's success. Some say that she has attempted to sabotage several of Miss Caroline's potential courtships."

"Rumors?" Nathan all but scoffed. "You should know how precarious such things are. How many outlandish tales concerning us and our friends have the Ton concocted out of whole cloth?" Though, if indeed true, such actions would certainly cool him to Miss Hughs, but there was no way of knowing for sure.

"Not all of them were outlandish. Rakehells to the bone the lot of us are."

"And don't I know it."

They shared a brief smile before Lockhart gestured to the doors. "Forget about these debutantes for now. The others are still waiting. You know the trouble Thurston might get into if left to his own devices for too long, and Kirkwood will be too busy taking his quizzing glass to the damn plants to rein him in."

"Alright," Nathan said with a laugh, thoughts of the enigmatic Miss Hughs set aside for the time being as the prospect of his friends making an utter cata-strophe out of the garden loomed. "Lead the way."

———

"Oh, yes, My Lord. I would love to dance the next set with you."

Arabella Hughs smiled tightly as her sister accepted yet another invitation for the evening. "Caroline," she said gently. "I believe you've already reserved that set for Lord Blemming."

Caroline turned around, her icy blonde curls glinting in the candlelight and deep brown eyes widening in surprise. "Oh, dear. You are right, Bella." She glanced back to the gentleman before them, the young heir to an earldom. "I apologize, My Lord."

"No need. It is a busy evening and perfectly easy to lose track of one's dance card." The young man looked awestruck as Caroline rewarded him with one of her winning smiles.

"My sister loves to dance, however."

Lord Eversham's pause was all Arabella needed to know regarding his opinion on the matter. "That is quite alright," she blurted. "I'm rather tired from the evening's exertions."

"But you've been standing here all night," Caroline protested.

"I'm tired," Arabella repeated, doing her best to hide any bite from her words. She'd not subject herself to a dance of pity, for Lord Eversham seemed quite clear in his reluctance. Caroline was the prize, not her. Not that she was in the mood for any kind of dancing, anyway.

"Quite right," Lord Eversham said, the relief in his voice palpable. "I've no wish to impose. Good evening,

Miss Hughs." His eyes strayed back to her sister and warmed anew. "Miss Caroline."

Caroline looked about ready to flutter her eyelashes as she watched Lord Eversham walk away. "Oh, drat. He would have been a good dance partner. So very handsome."

"You said that about Lord Edmund ten minutes ago."

"Yes, Lord Eversham," she replied with a sigh.

"Lord Edmund." Arabella tried to hide her smile of amusement.

Caroline waved her hand. "Eversham, Edmund, same difference. Both are wonderful specimens and so charming to boot. In fact, I'd say this Season has been rife with eligible gentlemen. Certainly better than the last with the likes of the mediocre Lord Lindsay."

Arabella stiffened at the name, that familiar, harsh blade of melancholy stabbing her chest. "Mediocre indeed," she mumbled.

But, seeming not to notice her sister's distress, Caroline continued. "So many eligible gentlemen, I am shocked you aren't as excited as I am about the possibilities."

Arabella herself had been just that one year ago. Though her come out year had been nothing spectacular, she'd received a few calls and one or two potential suitors. Last year, after having mastered her dancing and made improvements on her conversational skills, she'd been brimming with optimism. Except, last year had also been Caroline's debut, Arabella had quickly realized she held no chance next to a sister who'd been declared an incomparable from the moment she was introduced at court. With her delicate features, sweet disposition, and their grandfather's striking blonde hair, Caroline had taken the Ton by storm, with Arabella left to the wayside. And then rumors of her jealously surfaced, exaggerated tales of her prickly nature circulated, and she was well and truly doomed. One shining beacon of hope had surfaced, one that she now wished nothing more than to forget about. This season proved to be no better, though, for once, she was happy to fade in the background to nurse her broken heart in peace.

"Leave Arabella be, Caroline," their mother, Lady Drummel, stopped before them. "Was that Lord Eversham?" The analytical gleam in her eyes was plain to see. After it became apparent that Arabella's prospects were dead in the water, their enterprising mother had focused nearly all of her attention on Caroline in the hopes that the grand title she was likely to gain would make up for Arabella's dismal failure. Her mother's disinterest still stung, but not as severely as it once had. This was the unfortunate way of things, after all.

"Yes, he wanted a dance, but my card was full."

"Well," Lady Drummel smiled. "I'm sure he will come around again. Though I have another, better prospect for you, my dear."

"Oh?" Caroline smiled prettily.

"You'll see."

Moments later, a grandly fashioned lady with the

most regal bearing that Arabella had ever seen appeared behind her mother. "There you are, Felicity. I thought I recognized you in this crowd." The woman smiled, the expression dazzling despite her age.

Her mother turned and dipped into a curtsey. "Your Grace. It has been far too long."

The apparent duchess chuckled. "Please, do not be so formal with me."

"It is so wonderful to see you in London again. It's been what? Ten years?"

Ah, this was the Duchess of Milton, then. Arabella had heard of the famed lady's return to high society this season. A grieving widow who hadn't stepped a foot in London since the tragic loss of her husband and son, the woman's grand reentry had been the talk of the Ton for weeks. Most seemed convinced that her remaining child, the current duke, was hunting for a bride, and if the way Her Grace's face honed in on Caroline as she spoke with their mother, the assumption was likely not off the mark.

Their mother, either sensing the interest or expecting it, turned towards them with a sweep of her hand. "And these are my daughters. Caroline had her come out last year and has been a smashing success so far. Caroline, this is my dearest friend from finishing school, The Duchess of Milton."

She hadn't known of her mother boasting a friendship with the duchess, but then her mother hardly spoke to her at the best of occasions, even less so now that there was Caroline to focus on. It seemed Arabella wasn't even worthy of an introduction, though perhaps their mother was merely too excited at the prospect of snagging a duke to remember the oft forgotten daughter. The duchess, however, seemed to possess far better manners, for after gracing Caroline with a friendly smile and as her sister dipped, she shifted her attention. "And this lovely young lady?"

Arabella blinked a moment, wholly expecting the duchess to dote on Caroline, before lowering. "Arabella, Your Grace."

The duchess peered at her, before widening her smile. "Do you like dancing, Miss Hughs?"

"Very much. Though I've come to understand that liking to dance rarely equates to getting the opportunity." Oh, hell. She'd opened her fat mouth and said something prickly again. Arabella resisted the urge to slap a hand over her face. She'd been getting worse with her manners as of late, and while such a development normally served her well in this season's endeavor to remain outside of the marriage mart, acting in such a way before a duchess was a bit too much. The subtle pinch of her mother's hand on her side confirmed as much.

But before the duchess could react, Caroline and her sweetness swooped in to save the day. "Arabella is quite fatigued and unable to exert herself this evening, sadly. Why, just a moment ago, she was forced to turn down a most lovely young lord." Such words were why, no matter how much she was outshined, Arabella would never resent her sister. Caroline was as beautiful within as she was on the surface, her steadfast ally when she should by all rights disdain her as much as their mother.

"Oh, how unfortunate," the older woman lamented kindly. That odd light of interest towards Arabella faded, and Her Grace gazed kindly upon Caroline. "And how has your evening been, Miss Caroline? I hear there is practically a line to secure a dance with you at just about every ball this season."

Arabella turned from the conversation as Caroline made some elegant reply, their mother chiming in with praise at every opportunity. Though there had been that odd moment of attention from the Duchess, like with everyone else, her sister's shine had taken hold. It was likely for the best, lest Arabella let another quip slip and embarrass them all. A good impression with the woman might get Caroline an introduction to the Duke, and Arabella certainly would not hinder such an endeavor. It was herself she was sabotaging this year, not anyone else.

The trio continued to prattle, and Arabella surpressed a yawn of boredom whilst surveying the ballroom. She'd grown skilled at observation during her semi self-imposed wallflowerhood, and the Ton never disappointed with its hidden scandals. The amount of subtle assignations alone she could spot within an evening provided ample entertainment. Sadly, she noted with mild disappointment, the people milling about on this evening appeared as dull as the rest of tonight's ball.

Her eyes roved the floor until something, or rather someone, caught her eye. Tall and dark-haired, with deep blue eyes and a sculpted face, the person she spied from across the room epitomized the look of a classically handsome gentleman. He appeared happy and relaxed, chatting to his companion in a casual way that told her he cared little for the opinion of onlookers, and why would he? The striking similarity to the duchess, along with the fact that the man next to him was the infamous Lord Lockhart, whom only boasted of a handful of friends, could only mean that it was the Duke of Milton she surveyed. His Grace smiled at something Lockhart said, the expression lighting up his face to such a dazzling degree that it nearly blew her senses away. Perhaps Caroline hadn't been entirely wrong in her observations of this season's batch of gentlemen. Exciting possibilities, indeed.

Lord Lockhart gestured in their direction, and she suppressed an unwanted pinprick of envy as Milton's focus settled on Caroline. Arabella tore her gaze from him in disappointment, not interested in seeing another man mooning after her sister. She continued surveying the ballroom despite its dullness, her thoughts straying. No doubt the duke would hone in on Caroline, and she was sure that her mother was angling for an introduction, if the way the woman was all but extolling Caroline's virtues to the duchess were any sign. Arabella tightened her lips, attempting to suppress an amused smile as she heard her mother loudly and vividly describing Caroline's skill at embroidery. She couldn't blame her mother for trying so hard. Potentially snagging a duke was a rare opportunity for even the best of diamonds. Though, perhaps the duke was enamored already.

The smile broke through, and Arabella entertained herself with a momentary image of him doting in their drawing room like a besotted fool along with the rest of her sister's daily morning court. She dared a look back at Milton, wondering if he was still staring. Indeed, the man was looking in their direction, his lovely blue eyes focused squarely on... herself? Arabella blinked, wondering if she was imagining things. But no, his gaze was fixed firmly upon her person. Their eyes met, and he gave her a small nod, mouth quirking. She wasn't sure which was stronger: the utter bewilderment that a duke of all people would find anything of interest in her or the flush that threatened to overtake her at a duke of all people, finding anything of interest in her. But then, Lord Lockhart took Milton's attention once more, and the two fell into deep conversation. Arabella exhaled in relief as the men turned and walked off, obviously heading for some predetermined destination.

"Oh, drat." The duchess's voice took her attention once more. "I'm sorry, Felicity, but it looks like my son has wondered off somewhere. What a shame. I was hoping to bring him over here."

"He went with Lord Lockhart," Arabella supplied before her mother could speak.

"You recognized him, then?" The duchess looked at her with that odd expression once more.

"He is rather hard to miss." Arabella clamped her lips shut, that flush threatening to truly take hold. Thank goodness Milton had left, for she wasn't sure she could handle his presence up close, even if over the shoulder of her sister.

The Duchess chuckled. "Indeed, he is."

"Well," her mother interrupted. "I am sure there will be ample opportunity tonight to introduce us. And of course, Caroline would certainly be happy to receive Your Graces in our drawing room."

For someone who often scolded Arabella for impertinent words, her mother did, on occasion, prove herself to be just as uncouth. She couldn't think of a more embarrassingly direct hint. Lady Drummel nudged Caroline. "Wouldn't you, darling?"

Her sister needed no prompting. "Oh, yes, very much so."

"Well," the duchess smiled magnanimously. "We will look forward to seeing you, Miss Caroline." She nodded at Arabella. "And Miss Hughs."

Touched that the woman had made a gesture to include her, Arabella returned the expression. "Yes, Your Grace."

Soon after, the duchess took her leave, their mother staring mournfully at her form as she disappeared into the throng. "I do hope we can get you that introduction tonight, Caroline. You, a duchess. Can you imagine!"

"Whatever happens, happens, Mama," Caroline replied calmly, seeming just as amused as she at their mother's exuberance. She turned to Arabella, her curiosity palpable. "So, was he handsome?"

"Very much so, and he seemed kind, from a distance, at least. I am sure you will like him."

She clapped her hands. "Oh, how fun!"

Yes, she thought rather dreamily. Marvelous, indeed.

Chapter Two

As expected, they found Kirkwood deep in the home's expansive garden, crouched in front of a flower bush and peering at one leaf through his quizzing glass. Nearby, Thurmont held his pocket watch, tapping one foot and glaring at the doors with obvious impatience. His gaze narrowed as Nathan and Lockwood approached. "There you are. By God, I was about to give up and wander off. Kirkwood has been muttering nonsense about that bloody bush for the past fifteen minutes."

"It's a rare breed," the marquess replied, not looking up. "One I haven't seen up close in England."

"And there you have it," Thurmont said with a roll of his eyes. "I've been going mad from boredom, which quite says something about the state of this wretched ball if I'd rather subject myself to this pontification on the finer points of botany than mingle amongst the crowd."

"If only Derry were here, then there might be a modicum of excitement," Nathan said. Derry, or rather, Prince Derrick, was the fifth member of their motley crew and rarely in England these days, having duties within his own country to sort out. The five of them had formed a tight-nit friendship at Eaton and then Oxford, one that had never wavered to this day and was well known amongst the Ton, though not always for the best of reasons.

"That would be preferred." Kirkwood finally rose. "If only to hide from the marriage minded mamas. Speaking of which, I hear you plan on throwing yourself to the proverbial wolves this season."

"Yes, unfortunately."

Kirkwood shook his head. "Poor man. We'll be cheering you on from behind Derry."

"If he even gets here. The man was supposed to arrive a good two weeks ago. Likely got distracted and is wandering about somewhere again," Lockhart mused.

"Forget him for now," Thurmont interrupted with a wave of his hand as he closed in on the three. "I've come up with the most marvelous lark to get us through this abysmal season."

Nathan sighed. "Another bet, then?" Thurmont was fond of wagers, and more than a few of their group's scrapes had resulted from one of the earl's harebrained schemes.

"This one is perfectly harmless," Thurmont assured, likely sensing their hesitance.

Kirkwood frowned. "I doubt that."

"Well, I'm bored enough to do just about anything," Lockhart said. "And I'm sure Milton would like a distraction from his marriage predicament."

Nathan shrugged. "Fair enough." Surely a bit of fun to make the tedium bearable would be worth it. "Go on, Thurmont."

The earl grinned. "You're all going to dance. A waltz, specifically."

"What's the catch?" Nathan inquired, unease trickling up his spine. "There is always a catch with you. Not to brag, but half the ladies here would tumble over themselves for a dance with me and Lockhart alone."

Thurmont wagged his finger. "You're to dance, not just with any lady, but with one of my choosing."

"Let me guess," Kirkwood deadpanned. "You want us to convince someone difficult, don't you? One of those determined spinsters, I suppose?"

When Thurmont smiled in reply, Nathan rolled his eyes. "No, thank you. I've enough on my plate from the ladies who actually want to spend time with me. I'd rather not waste my time trying to cajole a prickly wallflower."

"I, for one, would love to take up the challenge," Lockhart said cheerily. "Those ladies deserve some attention, too."

"If the prize is worth it, perhaps," Kirkwood mused. "Though I warn you, it will take a good deal of temptation to get me out of this garden. There are many interesting blooms here I would like to inquire with our hostess about."

"Will you really not take part, Milton?" Thurmont looked about close to pouting.

"I will not."

"And if my Bellona was the reward?"

Nathan froze at the mention of the prized mare. The horse had yet to lose a race and was one of the most gorgeous thoroughbreds he'd ever laid eyes upon. She'd be the crown jewel of his stables, if only Thurmont would let her. Many times Nathan had offered increasingly outrageous sums for the horse, and every time he was refused. Frustrating, considering that Thurmont cared little for horse breeding, and had only purchased Bellona himself on a whim. If there was one thing in the world that would tempt him to take on this silly scheme, it was this. "Go on."

Thurmont grinned in triumph. "You get the dance within the next month, the horse is yours. No strings attached."

"Damn you, fine," Nathan grumbled, finishing the last of his champagne with a hard swallow. "How are we doing this?"

"You and Lockhart are up first, followed by Kirkwood and I."

"You're participating?"

"It's only fair. You all can pick the lady and the reward when my turn comes. And if Derry ever gets around to finally showing his face this season, I'll ask him if he wants a try."

"And if we fail?" Kirkwood said, ever the shrewd one of their group.

"Some humiliating task. I haven't quite decided yet. You'll just have to hope you don't fail, for you know how creative I can get."

Considering that the last time Thurmont came up with a punishment, the rest of them were nearly expelled from Eton, he took the threat seriously. Nathan still shivered at the memory of freezing his naked ass off in the middle of winter whilst half the dormitory jeered. "So, who are we to dance with?"

Thurmont put a finger to his chin. "Lets see." After a quiet moment, he thrust the finger towards Lockhart. "You will dance with Miss Cecily Balfour."

The color drained from the baron's face, his easy smile slipping. "Heavens, anything but her."

Nathan rose an eyebrow at the sight, wondering what on earth about the famous bluestocking would strike Lockhart so. True, her acerbic tongue was well known amongst the Ton, but surely the woman wasn't that unpleasant. Though, from the near sadistic smile on Thurmont's face, he must know something about Lockhart's experience with the spinster that the rest of them didn't. Making a note to ask Lockhart about it later, Nathan gave him a bracing slap on the shoulder. "Chin up, friend. Surely your charms will make it a breeze."

"The prize you have in mind for me better be worth it, Thurmont," Lockhart said, his voice foreboding.

"It will. I shall tell you soon. But first," Thurmont shifted his attention to Nathan, "your assignment."

"Go on," he replied. "I am curious to see who you have in mind for me after making such a perfect pick for Lockhart."

"Ha. Perfect," the baron repeated faintly, the terror in his voice obvious.

Ignoring him, Thurmont spoke. "Miss Arabella Hughs for you, Milton."

The small amount of tension within him eased. Leave it to Thurmont to pick a lady he was already interested in meeting, one who, by the way she seemed to look at him, would not at all be averse to an invitation. Bellona was his. "Wonderful. You'll lose that horse within the hour."

"Of course you give him her," Lockhart grumbled.

Thurmont frowned. "Is she not infamously unpleasant?"

"Perhaps, though I've never met the lady," Nathan said happily. "She seemed interested in me when I caught her staring. To be honest, I was hoping to meet her."

"Well, damn." The disappointment in Thurmont's voice was plain. "And here I thought I'd get to spend the entire house party watching you follow her around like a puppy."

Nathan perked up at the mention of the upcoming event, hosted by Thurmont's mother on the massive family estate next week. "She is attending?"

"I saw her and her sister amongst my mother's guest list, yes. Miss Balfour, too," Thurmont replied. "So when you inevitably fail tonight, Lockhart, just know you have time."

"Wonderful," Lockhart replied sarcastically.

"Don't get too cocky, Milton," Kirkwood said. "I daresay you may have quite the task ahead."

Nathan scoffed. "I'll have no problem securing a dance from Miss Arabella Hughs. In fact, I think it will make for a perfectly pleasant time." More than pleasant, if his initial judgment of the lady proved correct. An entertaining dance and the assurance of a prized animal? Perhaps tonight's ball wasn't so dull after all.

———

Arabella leaned against a pillar, watching as Caroline danced with a handsome earl. She was cheerful and vivacious as she twirled about, her partner obviously dazzled by the display. Dancing was Caroline's best skill, one that had served her well on the marriage mart. Even Arabella couldn't help but admire the ease with which her sister seemed to glide across the floor.

"I am going to the retiring room," her mother said. "Do behave yourself."

"Yes, mama," she replied dutifully, fighting the urge to roll her eyes. As if a wallflower like herself could get into any sort of mischief. She watched her mother disappear into the crowd and suppressed a yawn.

Standing around all night was fatiguing, and her toes were cramping from lack of movement. A walk to stretch her legs and work off the restless energy that had built within since spying the Duke of Milton was tempting. She glanced at Caroline once more as she twirled about in the jaunty quadrille. Their mother would return in time to receive her when the set was over. Decision made, Arabella left her spot and gingerly made her way along the edge of the ballroom. She'd heard that the home boasted of impressive gardens with a variety of rare and exotic plants. The prospect was enough of a diversion to entice her, along with the fact that the ballroom was downright sweltering in the summer heat. She was quite looking forward to the upcoming house party hosted by Lady Thurmont in a week's time, if only for the cool country air it would provide. After a few more minutes of picking through the throng, most of whom paid her no mind, she found the terrace doors she'd been looking for and quietly slipped from the ballroom and into the welcoming breeze of the outdoors. The garden was indeed impressive and, much to her delight, devoid of company. Before she could think better of it, Arabella made her way deeper into the greenery, admiring the lovely rosebushes along the way and taking in their luxurious scent.

"Don't get too cocky, Milton. I daresay you may have quite the task ahead," a male voice spoke from nearby.

Interest piqued at the mention of the duke,

Arabella crept closer to the commotion, peeking out from around a hedge. Milton and Lockhart were speaking with two other gentlemen, whom she could only assume were The Marquess of Kirkwood and Earl of Thurmont. The group was infamous among the Ton for their rakish exploits. Being cloistered in such a discreet corner of the garden meant that they were likely up to some sort of mischief. It would be wise to leave, lest they either detect her presence or she hear some lewd talk unsuitable for her ears. Ducking back behind the hedge, Arabella moved to retreat.

"I'll have no problem securing a dance from Miss Arabella Hughs. In fact, I think I will have a perfectly pleasant time," Milton said with an exaggerated scoff.

Arabella stopped in her tracks and nearly tumbled forward. Milton wanted to dance with her? Her cheeks warmed, stomach fluttering. Though she was still raw from the horrors of last season, surely one dance wouldn't hurt. A dance with a gentleman wholly interested in doing so with her. Her! She swallowed the giggle bubbling up her throat.

"Anything for a good piece of horseflesh. Eh, Milton?" one of the men teased. "I've heard she is incredibly prickly and unpleasant, so Kirkwood may be correct in his predictions of your failure. Remember, waltz by the deadline or Bellona stays in my stables."

"As if you even know what to do with a horse like that, Thurmont."

A horse. He was going to dance with her for a bloody horse.

Her smile dropped, the butterflies withering away and replaced by the heat of indignation. Perhaps that was why he'd been staring at her so intently earlier in the evening, analyzing his opponent to see how easily he would win what was quite obviously some ludicrous wager. Well, she thought with a huff as she quietly stormed away from the scene, if Milton thought she would simper and smile so easily, then he had another thing coming. Arabella reentered the ballroom, righteous fury having not abated in the slightest during the trek. Her mother and Caroline had already returned to their place, the latter peering curiously at her as she approached. "Are you alright, Arabella? You have a mighty flush."

"Perfectly fine," she bit out with a tight smile. "The stuffiness of the ballroom is overheating me."

Caroline frowned. "If you say so. Oh! Lord Derring is heading this way for our dance."

"Go on," Arabella replied kindly, even if her thoughts were anything but. She watched Caroline go out with her newest partner and simmered with every second that passed. The next dance was a waltz, one that she was reasonably sure was the last of the evening. No doubt Milton would make his move before then. She pictured him strolling in from the garden, chuffed at the thought of winning. His failure would be a delight to witness.

She scanned the ballroom, spotting the duke with ease. His handsome visage was hard to miss, and she was mortified at having been so fooled by such a charming facade. His mother had rejoined him, and the two were engaged in hushed conversation. Arabella tensed when he subtly pointed to her, his mother following the gesture. When the woman smiled and the two began walking towards her, she braced herself for the inevitable. Thank goodness her own mother had wondered off again after Caroline left for the dance, for Arabella was about to make a supreme ass of a duke in the middle of a crowded ballroom.

"Hello again, Miss Hughs," the duchess said as they stopped before her. "I am back with my Milton, as promised. Milton, may I introduce Miss Arabella Hughs."

Arabella curtseyed. "Your Grace."

He returned the gesture with an elegant bow. "Miss Hughs. A pleasure."

"I'll leave you to it, then." The duchess said with a knowing smile before leaving them. Poor, sweet woman.

He looked around. "You are alone."

Had she not just overheard him planning to use her to win a bloody horse, she might have been charmed by his elegant timbre, expertly laced with just the barest hint of masculine interest. But now, Arabella knew it was merely a facade to get what he wanted from her.

Just like Edmund.

She swallowed down the bitter memories and pasted on a bland smile. "Unfortunately, both my mother and Caroline are occupied at the moment, though my sister will return after this set."

"That is alright," he replied, his voice as smooth as velvet. "Will you do me the honor of the next waltz?"

Oh, how she almost wished he was sincere, that the anticipation in his sapphire eyes had anything to do with her rather than the prize he was trying to win. For the briefest of moments, Arabella pretended it was true and basked in the warmth coursing through her at the thought. She smiled, beamed really, and gave him just about the sweetest face she could muster. "No."

He cheerily extended his arm. "Excellent, let us—wait, what did you just say?" The perplexed frown on his face was just about the funniest thing she'd seen in her life.

"No," Arabella repeated. "And it will always be no. Sadly, that horse shall remain forever out of reach.".

Milton swallowed. "Oh."

She frowned at last. "Oh, indeed."

To his credit, the man flushed. "You overheard our conversation."

She nodded. "I must say, having my worth be compared to a horse is about the least flattering thing I think I've ever heard said about myself, and there have been many unflattering things said about me."

Though they likely couldn't hear the particulars of the conversation, people were staring nonetheless. It wasn't every day one saw a duke flushing nearly down to his toes in mortification. No doubt there would be much speculation as to the cause, likely every tale blaming her. Arabella was far from caring. Watching him gape like a fish and struggle for a reply was more than gratifying to her wounded pride.

He grimaced. "Would you believe me if I said that I did not mean any offense? Truly, the horse is spectacular, but that is not the only reason I sought you out."

Arabella rose an eyebrow as he continued to fidget. "You're telling me you would have asked me to dance, regardless?"

"Yes," he declared, the sincerity in his eyes taking her aback. But then she reminded herself that the man was a proven liar, and his membership amongst that infamous group of rogues brought her back to reality.

"That must be one lovely horse for you to keep humiliating yourself like this."

His shoulder's slumped. "You don't believe me."

"No." Arabella suppressed the giggle working its way up her throat at the sight of him looking so pathetic in front of the crowd. She'd have hell to pay later once her mother got wind of this, but it was worth it for her petty revenge. His hand was still outstretched from the earlier invitation, and she couldn't help a small grin of mirth from slipping through. "Good evening, Your Grace," she proclaimed, loud enough for the surrounding guests to hear, before turning on her heel and striding away, leaving him stranded there like an utter fool as the first notes of the waltz began. If her prospects were dim before this scene, they were certainly dire now. Which was for the best, she assured herself.

Arabella was tired of noblemen and their deceptions.

Chapter Three

Nathan rose early, as he often did, despite arriving at Thurmont's estate well into last evening. One of the horses had thrown a shoe, forcing him and his mother to wait the delay out in a nearby village. And once they'd finally arrived, Thurmont had insisted on taking him aside for a night of brandy and billiards. Kirkwood and Lockhart wandered down in spite of the late hour, and the four of them had a bit of a raucous evening. Nathan rubbed the side of his mildly aching head with a yawn and peered out of his bedchamber window towards the emerging dawn. He always left his curtains open so the light would awaken him, lest he miss his daily morning ride. Every sunrise, barring some catastrophe, Nathan would saddle his horse and be off to explore wherever he was, whether that be the paths of Hyde park or the meandering fields of the countryside. The routine provided time to relax and contemplate whatever troubles he had with a level head. Today, he had a myriad of troubles to contemplate, most of them stemming from a certain wallflower.

"Bloody bold chit," he muttered to himself as he stood from his bed. Nathan could still feel the burn of his cheeks as she delivered that brilliant set down and left him gaping like a fool in the middle of the ballroom for half the Ton to gawk at. His estimation of her wit had been right on the mark, and he'd deserved to be a victim of it. Nathan was no Lockhart, but he was still confident in his affinity for charm. And yet, in front of those scorching brown eyes and the impertinent smirk curling her red lips, he'd been tongue tied and unable to salvage the situation. What was supposed to have been an easy win and an enjoyable waltz with a fascinating lady had turned into an utter disaster, one he would have to rectify soon lest he lose the lady's esteem entirely.

After dressing and procuring some bread from a surprised scullery maid, Nathan made his way to the stables. "I have it, lad," he said brightly to a drowsy stable hand as the boy made to grab the tack. Nathan preferred to saddle horses himself, enjoying the relaxing routine and time to bond with his mount. He strode to Highwind's stable, the glossy black stallion stirring at his approach. "And how is my favorite boy today?" he cooed, setting down the load to give the horse a gentle pat on his nose. Highwind leaned into the hand with a gentle chuff, but the stamping of his hooves belied the horse's impatience to be out. "Yes,

yes," Nathan said with a chuckle. "I'll have you ready to go soon enough. It'll be a nice long ride today, for I have much to think about."

After fitting him out, Nathan led Highwind out. They passed Bellona's stable, and he slowed down to admire the striking mare. Having a close look at her shining chestnut coat and well muscled proportions, Nathan was all the more determined to win. "See her?" he said with a pat on his horse's neck. "That is your future bride. Oh, your foals will be sublime. I cannot wait." Highwind flicked a brief glance to the mare before jerking his neck to tug Nathan along, his disinterest clear.

Ah, well. There would be plenty of time to get the two acquainted once he had them in his pastures, and he *would* have Bellona in his pastures. Rather than a deterrent, as Miss Hughs had likely hoped, Nathan's spectacular failure had only emboldened him further. Thurmont's snickering in the days that followed bolstered his determination to best the earl even more. This house party would be his best, perhaps the only chance to sway Miss Hughs to his cause. While his charm had undoubtedly failed, surely there was another means with which to convince the lady. He just needed to think.

"Alright, my good boy," he said with a gentle stroke on Highwind's mane before hauling himself into the saddle. "Let us go for a good long outing, yes?"

For the next hour, Nathan all but tore through the expansive lands, the great thunder of Highwind's hooves blanking his mind and sweeping his every worry away. There was just something about the country that invigorated his riding far more than any brief excursions to the London parks ever could. The hobby had served him well in the wake of his inheritance. It had been one of the few balms to those dark days ten years ago, when the only other thing filling his mornings was an empty breakfast table and the silence of his mother's locked door.

But these were better days now, and Nathan was thankful that his primary concerns were limited to marriage woes and stubborn spinsters. Thoughts of the former soured his mood a bit, and he slowed down to meander along the crest of an impressive hill. In the distance, he spotted Thurmont's house, a towering marble monstrosity that was a testament to the Harding family's decadence. He and his friends had spent many a summer rampaging through the extensive halls like the hellions they were. It was those fond memories and Thurmont all but begging for company during what was obviously a matchmaking party that had convinced him to accept the invitation. The duchess expected him to take some of the ladies here as serious contenders, had said as much on the way up. It was a task he was not looking forward to, as necessary as it was, though he supposed this way was better than morosely wandering a ballroom. But such thoughts were for later. He had a good two weeks up here, after all. For now, he would come up with a plan to get that horse.

Nathan continued along the hilltop at a leisurely pace, eyeing the inviting lake in the distance with anticipation. It seemed the idyllic spot to allow Highwind a refreshing drink and for himself to take a breather from the exhilaration of the ride. He'd spent many an hour as a young boy frolicking in the crystalline waters with the others, and the site was one of the reasons that Thurston's estate had been their group's favored place to stay during the summers between terms. He drew closer to the lake and soon realized that he was not alone. A young woman sat at the bottom of the hill, a sketchbook perched in her lap as she drew. Not wanting to bother a single lady alone and unchaperoned, Nathan made to urge Highwind along, until the woman turned her head enough that he could see the outline of a familiar chin and cheeks beneath the bonnet she wore. He'd recognize those fascinating lips anywhere.

Miss Hughs.

What delightful fortune, Nathan thought with a secret smile. He pulled Highwind's reins to cancel the horse's flight. Now was his chance to rectify the disaster of last week. If only he'd actually been able to come up with a reasonable plan during the long ride.

———

Arabella rose from her bed with a loud yawn. They'd arrived at the house party yesterday, everything going smoothly. Luckily for Arabella, her mother had opted to share a room with Caroline, leaving her alone with one of the two chambers they'd been provided. Unlike the other two, she liked to rise early. Lady Thurmont had mentioned a beautiful lake only a mile or so from the manor, and Arabella wanted to get there in time to see the sun rising over the vista. Sunrises were her favorite things to paint, and the thought of having several stunning paintings to create had been one of the reasons she'd agreed to the house party in the first place. Potentially finding a husband out of the many single gentlemen in attendance was Caroline's task, not hers. After dressing and gathering her sketchbook, Arabella trotted happily through the silent halls and down the stairs. Only the servants were up at this hour, and several of them glanced at her with surprised curiosity. The air was refreshingly cool once she left the house, the heat of the summer day not yet taking hold this early in the morning. Following the directions given to her by Lady Thurmont, she made her way down the path leading to the lake. A young woman appeared on the horizon, walking in the opposite direction.

"Oh! Good morning," the lady called with a cheery wave. "I did not realize anyone else would be up at this hour." The woman came closer, revealing the face under the brim of her bonnet.

Arabella smiled cordially. "Miss Cecily Balfour, correct?" A few years her senior and often mocked over her passion for the sciences, the spinster was firmly on the shelf and seemed to prefer things that way, if her less than regular attendance at London events was any sign.

"Yes," Miss Balfour replied with her own friendly grin. "I do not believe we have met, but you are Miss Arabella Hughs."

"My reputation precedes me, I see."

She laughed. "As does mine, apparently." She gestured to Arabella's sketchbook. "Off to the lake?"

"I was hoping to catch the sunrise."

"It was breathtaking when I left. You won't be disappointed."

Arabella wondered what reason Miss Balfour would have for going to the lake herself, if not to sketch, but she wouldn't pry. "I am glad to hear it. Let us speak again soon."

"I would like that very much, Miss Hughs. Good morning to you, then." With one last chipper wave, Miss Balfour continued on her way. At least she would have a friendly acquaintance to converse with for the next two weeks during the tedium of socializing. Arabella couldn't hide in her room or wander the estate forever, after all.

After a few more minutes of walking, she reached her destination. The lake did not disappoint. Surrounded by scores of wildflowers, and almost seeming to glow under the light of the rising sun, the scene would make for a lovely painting. Two swans swam leisurely along the far shore, a charming addition to the idyllic image. Happy with the potential, Arabella plopped down and began her first sketch. Art had always been a wonderful distraction, and she'd delved even deeper into the hobby over the past year. Better to focus on the curve of a line or pontificate on the correct shading of a particular tree rather than dwell in unpleasant memories.

And yet, no matter how much she focused on the lake, images of a certain duke and his ludicrous display last week still pushed their way into her thoughts. She'd not heard hide nor hair of him since that ball, much to her relief. Perhaps the fickle man had already given up on the damn horse if he'd gone so long without even attempting another overture. And now she was out in the country and would be so for some time. No doubt he would grow bored with the sport. Arabella should have been relieved, but a part of her could admit to a small amount of disappointment. He'd seemed so determined, and she had wondered what kind of foolish antics the man would resort to, if only for her entertainment. The set down she'd delivered at the ball had been supremely satisfying. A shame that there wouldn't be another opportunity to do so again. Though, her mother might well and truly murder her were she to go through with it. Her previous antics had earned a sound scolding, with her mother despairing of the duke ever showing himself again. Arabella settled more comfortably in the grass with a happy sigh. No matter what the coming months might bring, at the very least she would have some piece and quiet for the time being. No need to deal with his smiling face, those captivating eyes, or that sultry voi—"Ho! Is that the lovely Miss Hughs I spy so early in the morning?"

No. Impossible.

Arabella whipped her head toward the familiar voice, stomach dropping upon confirming that it had indeed been the Duke of Milton she'd heard. He sat upon a glorious black mount atop one of the grassy hills, looking far too lovely for her liking. If she didn't despise him at the moment, Arabella might have had him stay right where he was for her to sketch. With his windswept dark hair, shapely lips curving as if the mere sight of her had made his day, he would have made for an utterly romantic painting. If only his personality matched that stunning tableau. She groaned inwardly as he steered his horse towards a nearby tree. What in the world was he even doing here?

"Why, I was invited. Thurmont is one of my best friends, after all," he said, stopping before her. Blast, she'd said that last part aloud. She wasn't sure whether to be relieved or concerned that he hadn't seemed to take the slightest offense to her acerbic tone.

Repeating her mother's scolding like a mantra in her head, Arabella donned a tense smile. "Yes, of course. Good morning, Your Grace."

"Did you not know the guest list, Miss Hughs? I was under the impression that most ladies made sure to know the names of every single gentleman in atten-dance at these affairs, as that is rather the point of going, or so my mother tells me. I'm not very well versed in the marriage mart as I should be." He finished that line with a depreciating smile, and it angered her that she was charmed by his modesty.

"I did not know who was coming, no. That is more my sister's job at the moment." She tried to keep the bitterness out of her voice, but it slipped into the statement, regardless. This was, technically, her first house party as a single debutante, as there hadn't been such an opportunity during her come out. Two years ago she might have been over the moon at the thought of a potential romance in the idyllic countryside, as Caroline had been nearly all week. But that time had come and gone for her. "I am here to enjoy the country sights. London is stifling and this social season has been dull."

"Now there is something we can agree on." He glanced down at her lap and the sketchbook perched atop it. "Sketching, I see. May I join you?"

"I suppose. I know you'll just foist your company on me, anyway." Arabella clamped her mouth shut after the statement. Her mother was going to kill her.

"Oh, come now, Miss Hughs. I'm not that much of a beast, am I?"

She smiled serenely, setting down her sketchpad lest she accidentally crunch the paper in her hand. "Of course not, Your Grace."

"Oh goodness, no. That false kindness will not do," he declared as he dismounted. His voice carried across the lake as he secured his mount. "It is rather unnerving, actually, when I know you despise me at the moment." He trotted down the hill, that friendly grin not leaving his face. "And yes, I will foist my company on you."

She nearly laughed despite herself. "Arrogant man."

"Comes with the dukedom, I'm afraid." He all but plopped down beside her, leaning back to lounge against the hill. "I promise I won't tell anyone how rude you've been so far today." He furrowed his handsome brow. "Actually, best not tell anyone at all about this little meeting of ours."

The words were wise, though she was reasonably certain no one else would be out and about at this hour to come upon them. She wondered what he would do were they to be compromised. Ruin her? Marry her? She tried to conjure the image of them at the altar together but wiped the thought aside as quickly as it had come. What a ridiculous notion. "Agreed."

Arabella turned back to her sketchbook, waiting for him to speak. A few moments passed in silence, and she paused her work. "What is it you wish to say to me?"

"Haven't figured it out yet."

She darted a glance at him. Milton lounged against the hill, hands behind his head and one knee propped up. The riding breeches he wore hugged his muscular thighs most becomingly, and she quickly averted her gaze back to the sketch. "I'm not sure there is anything for you to figure out. I've made my feelings on the matter quite clear, and I assumed you understood that well."

"I understand nothing at all about you, actually."

"It almost sounds like you want to get to know me," she replied flippantly. As if he would find anything of interest about her.

"I do," he replied. "To be honest, I've found you interesting from the moment I saw you."

She swallowed, stomach fluttering, but continued to draw. "Was that before or after I was singled out for this silly bet?" The answer was obvious, and his marked silence after the question only confirmed her suspicions.

And then he inhaled and spoke, his voice slow and almost hesitant. "Before."

The pencil almost fell from her hand before she steeled herself once more. "I don't believe you."

Although she wasn't looking at him, she knew he was shrugging. "That's your prerogative, I suppose."

"It's the truth." Arabella looked at him once more, fixing a glare on his lounging form. That he could be so serene whilst driving her nerves to distraction was almost intolerable.

He looked back, his blue eyes clear and steady. "I spied you across that ballroom well before even knowing about the bet. You seemed an interesting person. Really," he continued with a slight note of exasperation, "you do not need to be envious of your sister, beauty that she is."

The swell of flattered pleasure that had begun

during the start of his statement died a swift and bitter death. "You think me jealous of her?" Like the rest of them. If he was trying to lighten her view towards him, he was failing miserably.

"Are you?"

"I will not dignify that with an answer." She smacked her sketchbook shut and rose.

He scrambled up behind her. "Miss Hughs, wait." His voice was contrite, but she'd already lost what little patience for him she'd had.

"Good day, Your Grace." Propping her sketchbook under one arm, she strode away in the most dignified manner she could muster, hoping to look more like a regal queen rather than the wounded wallflower she was, and ignored the prickle of disappointment when his footsteps did not follow.

CHAPTER FOUR

"WELL, that went about as bad as it could have," Nathan muttered to himself as he watched Miss Hughs all but flee down the lakeside path. Their little chat had been going well, so well that he was reasonably sure he'd come close to convincing her to go along with the bet. It seemed, however, that her sister's success on the marriage mart was a sore topic, sore enough to upend her mood entirely. He wondered if the rumors of her jealously were indeed true. But then, that mournful look in her gaze whilst she spoke seemed far from such an acidic emotion. For the briefest of moments, before he'd blurted that awful response, he'd considered kissing the melancholy right of her face. But that was, perhaps, even worse than the accidental insult he'd given her. Flirtations with debutantes were precarious things when one didn't have courtship in mind.

Thoughts in a jumble, Nathan made his way back

to Highwind. He set off down the fields, determined to make the most of his limited time. Despite its earlier effectiveness, the relaxing thrum of the ride did nothing to clear his mind, and by the time Nathan finally made his way back to the house, he was no closer to a solution to his admittedly self imposed problem. If only he hadn't been so damned impetuous during their conversation, he might have achieved his aim.

"Milton, there you are," his mother exclaimed as he strode into the foyer after changing from his riding clothes. Dressed in a cheery yellow day dress and wearing a bright smile, she looked happier than he'd seen her in some time. No doubt the break from London and the myriad of other guests to socialize with was the cause of her good mood. His mother always shone the brightest around others, and Nathan would do whatever she bloody hell wanted if it meant keeping that serene glow on her.

"Were you searching for me, mother? I was on my morning ride."

"It is nearly luncheon, my boy. Was the ride truly so invigorating?"

Nathan smiled back. "The most invigorating I've had in some time, actually." In more ways than one. But those were dangerous thoughts to humor if he was to keep himself steady for the rest of the trip and execute his required tasks, one of which he was sure was the reason his mother was looking for him. "What did you need of me?"

She looped her arm around his as they made their way to the garden where the first luncheon of the party was to be held. Her voice was quiet as she spoke. "I have someone I would like you to meet."

He raised an eyebrow. "Matchmaking already? We've barely been here twelve hours."

"I am nothing if not efficient," she replied. "I had actually hoped to introduce her to you at the ball last week. She is the daughter of a dear friend of mine, though I'm sure you have heard much of her. Miss Caroline Hughs is a spectacular diamond."

"Ah, the sister of Miss Hughs."

"I had hoped to introduce you to both of them at that ball, but alas, only the elder had been available. I had thought Miss Hughs to be kind, but it seems I misjudged her character, what with that scene she started. What did she say to make you so befuddled?"

"Please, do not blame her. The incident was entirely my fault." Not that the gossips thought so. He could only hope the poor woman's prospects hadn't been completely ruined for the season because of a set down he entirely deserved.

His mother peered at him, a look he was long familiar with when trying to hide his mischief as a boy. "What did you do, Milton?"

"Nothing," he blurted. "I merely misspoke and accidentally insulted her."

From the look she gave him, the woman didn't believe him for a second. "I see." She shook her head. "No matter. I will introduce you to Miss Caroline, and perhaps Miss Highs will also be there. If you insulted her, then you have time to apologize. No doubt she's already given her sister an unfavorable impression of you if you were indeed the one to cause that scene."

"I will be sure to do so," he said. His mother needn't know that the apology had already been attempted just this morning, or that he'd bumbled the interaction up enough to warrant a second one.

Unfortunately, or perhaps fortunately, Miss Hughs was nowhere to be found once they emerged into the garden. Several tables filled with refreshments had been set up, with most of the guests milling about them. He spotted Miss Caroline's platinum hair from the distance. "There she is, mother."

Lady Drummel brightened as she spotted them heading over, giving her daughter a not-so-subtle tap on the shoulder. "Your Graces," she greeted as they stopped before them.

HIs mother nodded with a bright smile. "Hello, Felicity. I was so relieved to hear that you and your daughters were on the guest list. Here is my Milton, as promised. Milton, Lady Drummel and her daughter, Miss Caroline Hughs."

"A pleasure," he said, giving both women a kiss on their hands. Up close, Miss Caroline was a sight to behold, indeed. Her delicate, doll-like features and glowing blonde hair gave her an almost ethereal sort of beauty that made it no mystery why she had half of the Ton all but eating out of her palm.

She stared at him with wide, ice-blue eyes as he

rose, dainty lips quirking with a small, shy smile. "Your Grace." Her voice was soft, with an almost breathless quality. "I have heard much about you."

His mother gave him a subtle, encouraging look as she conversed with Lady Drummel. Taking the obvious hint, command really, Nathan held out his arm. "Would you care for a stroll around the gardens? I know much about their construction, if such things interest you."

"I would love nothing more, Your Grace," she replied, her small smile widening with pleasure. It was a truly dazzling sight, and were he a lesser man, Nathan might have decided on his duchess right there. But he knew better than to judge one's character by their surface appearance, and if Miss Caroline was truly a good fit for him, he would have to take the time to discern the personality under that glorious veneer.

He could almost see Lady Drummel already planning the wedding in her head as she gave her daughter a nudge. "Go on, Caroline. I'll just be here with Her Grace. We have much catching up to do."

"Do take your time, Milton," his mother said. "I haven't spoken to Lady Drummel in some years." That she seemed to favor Caroline as a contender was more than apparent. Nathan trusted his mother's judgement. If she thought that Miss Caroline to be a solid possibility, he would entertain the notion, at least.

"Shall we?" he said.

The debutante grasped his arm in a gentle whisper of a grip. "Lead the way."

Miss Caroline was a charming conversation partner, nodding in all the right places and seeming to have a genuine interest in the things he was saying rather than merely attempting to appear so, even providing her own astute observations when warranted. She was pleasant.

Only pleasant.

He stared at her as she inquired about the origins of the garden fountain and tried his best to stir some excitement for her within him, but nothing came. Not even the tiniest pinprick if interest made itself known.

"Oh, there is Arabella, Your Grace," Miss Caroline said before he could respond to her earlier questions. Emphasizing the observation, she pointed at the door. As if he needed help locating Miss Hughs whenever she entered the room. A flush of embarrassment coursed through him at the memory of his words that morning. He would need to find a way to speak to her, hopefully before the luncheon was up.

"Perhaps we should greet her?" He suggested. "Your mother seems preoccupied." Indeed, Lady Drummel was gushing over something with his mother, no doubt Miss Caroline, and hadn't seemed to notice her eldest daughter's entry. Miss Hughs was sipping a glass of lemonade, and for a moment he admired the way the light of the afternoon sun shone over her golden hair before realizing something was amiss. Her frame was stiff, the glass lightly shaking in her hands, and she seemed on the verge of tears.

"Yes, let us go," Miss Caroline murmured, not

looking at him but at Miss Hughs, her mouth forming a thin line. She quickened her pace, clutching his arm tight as if to drag him along with her to their destination. Miss Hughs glanced over, spotting them almost immediately. Her face paled, but before he could even think of giving her some sort of reassuring expression, she turned on her heel and hastened to the door.

"Is everything alright?" he asked, watching her form disappear inside.

"The crowd might have overwhelmed her, I'm afraid." Miss Caroline looked back up at him, her smile more false than before. "Let us return to my mother. I've seen enough of the garden."

Something was afoot concerning Miss Hughs, but he knew better than to pry into what seemed to be personal family business. He dropped off Miss Caroline, ignoring his mother's inquiring glance. "Excuse me a moment, ladies," he said with a polite smile before walking off. There may be nothing he could do about whatever troubled Miss Hughs this afternoon, but he could certainly make up for his own contribution to her poor day. Striding back into the house, he waved down a passing footman. "Pardon, lad, might I borrow you for a task?"

———

Arabella rested her hand on the knob of her chamber door, debating whether to attend luncheon or plead a headache. After that disastrous and infuriating conversation with Milton, she'd stormed back to the manor and stewed in her room for the rest of the morning. How dare the man ruin what should have been a wonderful, idyllic sketching session with his obnoxious presence and rude intimations. For some bizarre reason that she still couldn't quite understand, Arabella had thought him different from the others. But no, it seemed he believed her a jealous spinster, covetous of her sister's success and willing to sabotage things if given the opportunity. A part of her, a minuscule part, had begun to believe his words at the ball. Now, however, it was more than apparent that his only interest in knowing her was getting that waltz and the prized mare that went with it. She shouldn't be disappointed, yet a stubborn part of her was still bitterly hurt by the revelation.

Someone knocked on the door. "Arabella?" her mother's voice sounded from the other side.

"Yes, I am here."

Her mother opened the door, face pinched with a serious expression. "I wish to speak with you before heading down for luncheon. I have plans that would be much easier with your help."

"Plans?" Unease gathered within. Whenever her mother had some sort of scheme, usually involving setting Caroline up with some gentleman or other, things rarely went well.

Lady Drummel nodded. "I'll have Milton for Caroline."

"Milton?" she replied, incredulous. But then, who

else would her mother set her sights on? Milton was the catch of the season and Caroline was *Caroline*. It'd be the match of the decade. Something heavy she couldn't identify settled in the pit of her stomach.

"Why do you look so surprised?" Lady Drummel narrowed her eyes. "Unless you think you have a chance of snagging him yourself."

"Of course not." It was laughably ludicrous, but that her mother was the one, of all people, to point out her inadequacy seemed an extra blow to her already crumbling self-esteem, not that she'd give Lady Drummel the satisfaction of knowing that, or anyone for that matter. Stomping down her unpleasant emotions, Arabella straightened her spine. "I merely think that he would not be a good fit for her."

"Nonsense. He is a duke."

"That's not what I—"

"Besides, I've already discussed the match with Her Grace. We are both thrilled at the prospect, and she will do whatever she can to see it through. If she thinks it is a good idea, then I cannot see how your opinion on the matter would hold any weight."

Her opinions had never held weight on anything, as far as Lady Drummel was concerned, but Arabella knew better than to start another argument. They had enough of those as it was. But that didn't mean she would aid in this ridiculous scheme. "If you have Her Grace on board, then I fail to see how I would be needed."

"Are you really so jealous that you won't even help your sister make this brilliant match?"

Oh, for heaven's sake. If it wouldn't get her in trouble, Arabella's eyes would have rolled into the back of her skull. "I'm going downstairs." She shouldered past her mother and out the door.

"I am not done speaking with you," Lady Drummel called at her back.

Arabella ignored her and kept going, lest her irritation simmer over. The last thing she needed was for someone to see her and her mother arguing in the middle of the hall, least of all Caroline. Rather than head straight to the garden where the meal was being held, Arabella went in the opposite direction after heading down the stairs. The house was almost labyrinthian in its sheer size, and there were many winding halls for her to explore whilst she cooled her head.

By the time she'd found her way back, a good half hour had already passed, and the luncheon was well underway. There was a moment's anxiety at being so late, before she remembered it was likely no one would care, anyway. Most had paid her no mind during these first few days, and Arabella was convinced that her invitation had been a mere courtesy rather than any desire for her presence. Lady Thurmont had made it no secret that she was hunting for a bride for her reluctant son, hence why so many single ladies were in attendance. The desperation with which the countess was trying to get him leg-shackled was well known amongst the Ton. Amusingly, Lord Thurmont had made himself rather scarce this week, only seeming to be found in the company of his friends when he wasn't outright hiding. Lady Thurmont and her mother would get along well, she thought with a chuckle to herself. She imagined the two huddled in a corner somewhere, exchanging notes on the best schemes to marry their respective children off.

The ridiculous picture was enough to lighten her mood, and by the time she'd reached the garden, Arabella was feeling almost pleasant. Let them think her a jealous, bitter woman. She would show herself to be having a wonderful time despite them. If her mother wanted to parade around Caroline in front of Milton, then she wouldn't care one bit.

That internal proclamation, bold when she'd crossed the threshold into the afternoon sun, wavered the moment she laid eyes on the assembled guests. Her mother was chatting with The Duchess of Milton, an enthused gleam shining in her eyes that likely had far more to do with her matchmaking plans than whatever the duchess was saying. No doubt she was gushing Caroline's praises. As for Caroline...

Arabella scanned the crowd, heart sinking once she spotted her sister on Milton's arm. They made for a handsome pair as they strolled about the garden, Caroline's smile as she listened to whatever pretty words Milton was uttering as beautiful as ever. A sudden, heartbreaking sense of déjà vu hit her at the sight.

Arabella had been taken on a lovely stroll around a luxurious picnic much like this one. With *him*.

Reminding herself of her earlier vow, Arabella plucked a glass of lemonade from a passing tray and sunk into the corner of the gathering, taking a deep breath to calm the sudden wave of heartache. As she'd expected, no one payed her any mind, many seeming more fixated on her sister and the duke, leaving her alone to sort herself in peace. Damn that disloyal bastard for still having such a hold on her. She took a bracing gulp of her beverage as Caroline's melodic laugh sounded nearby. It was ridiculous, really, to be so bothered. Milton was not the same, not in the slightest, at least being relatively upfront about his attention towards her being for that damn horse and the horse alone. The proof of that was right before her in all its perfect, fitting glory. And yet, somehow, that observation only made her heart sink ever more deep into the pits of her belly.

'Why would I have any interest in you, Miss Hughs?' The memory of Lord Lindsay's words bounced around in her mind. She inhaled as her throat thickened. It'd been months since she'd had such an episode and it was infuriating that her emotions would spring up on her in the middle of a crowded garden. Her heart seized as she realized Caroline and Milton were heading her way, the knowing concern etched on her sister's face plain. Not wanting to humiliate herself in front of the duke, especially after their horrid exchange earlier in the day, Arabella turned and all but

fled from the garden. It was only when she crossed the threshold into the foyer, calm save for the occasional servant passing by, that she allowed herself to relax. She walked up the stairs at a sedate pace, secure in the knowledge that no one would follow her, leaving her to settle herself in peace. Caroline wouldn't pursue her, despite likely knowing she was remembering Lord Lindsay again, as Arabella preferred to be left alone during moments such as these. By the time she'd returned to her room, the ache had settled, and Arabella spent the next few hours perfecting her lakeside sketch to further calm her roiling mind. The stress of the party and dealing with Milton must have gotten to her, making her vulnerable to dangerous memories, embarrassing as it was.

The afternoon ticked by, her mood improving by the hour. The sketch was coming along nicely, and she was confident that a lovely painting was in the works upon her return to London. She would have to be sure to visit the site a few more times to catch the entirety of its beauty. Arabella was just about to set her drawing aside for the day and ring for some tea when a knock sounded on the door. "One moment," she called and set down her work.

Upon opening the door, she was confused to see a young footman behind it, a folded note in his hands. "I have instructions to give this to you, m'am," he said, holding out the note.

She took it with a tentative thanks and closed the door, turning the paper back and forth. "Oh!" she gasped as something purple slipped from the folds and tumbled in front of her feet. "How peculiar." She picked up the sprig of lavender, twirling it in her fingers, before setting it down on her bed and unfolding the note.

I sincerely hope my rude behavior this morning was not the cause for your distress at luncheon. I beg for forgiveness if so, and I will grovel for an apology at your earliest convenience if that is indeed the case.

A small laugh forced its way out of her as she finished the note, and Arabella set it down with an amused shake of her head. It seemed the Duke of Milton wasn't as much of a cad as she'd initially thought, or he was so full of himself to assume that all her troubles must revolve around him. Regardless, she was touched in spite of herself. "Silly man."

CHAPTER FIVE

"HE WAS SO handsome and charming, Bella. Nothing at all like you described him to me."

Arabella eyed her sister from her place at the armoire as she adjusted the comb nestled in her hair. "You seemed to get along well with His Grace, from what I could see," she said indulgently.

"Oh, he was lovely and squired me throughout the entire gardens. I had such a pleasant time," Caroline all but gushed. Her sister hadn't brought up Arabella's flight from luncheon since coming in, much to her own relief. Caroline treating her no differently, as if nothing were wrong and she hadn't nearly embarrassed herself in front of an entire house party, was far more soothing than the hugs and concerned inquiries that had already been performed to exhaustion in the past year.

"Will you set your cap for him, then?" She tried to ignore the twisting in her gut at the thought. Really, there was no reason to feel such. It was only natural that the duke would gravitate towards Caroline, who held all the qualities needed for the perfect duchess. And he was still annoying, even if that thoughtful apology had softened her opinion to a small degree. The note was still nestled in a drawer, along with the lavender that had come with it.

"You should have gone with the sapphires instead of the emeralds. They look better with your golden shade of hair," Caroline chided, bypassing the question. It was no matter, for she wouldn't spend so much time gushing about Milton as she had for the past twenty minutes if she wasn't taking him seriously as a candidate. Then again, her sister admired gentlemen often, but never seemed to pursue things beyond a passing interest. Whether the duke also fell into that category remained to be seen.

Arabella adjusted the emerald comb once more. "It is perfectly acceptable. Besides, the sapphires look striking in your own hair."

"Everything looks striking in my hair," Caroline deadpanned. "Honestly, it can be annoying." She approached the armoire and lowered her head beside Arabella's, turning it side to side so that the jewels glittered in her hair. "I often feel like a fussy peacock when mother insists I dress my hair this way."

Arabella covered her snort with her hand. "That is not true."

Caroline playfully rolled her eyes. "Yes, it is, and you know it. You wouldn't have laughed otherwise."

"I'm sorry," she replied with a mild giggle.

"I look far better in simpler fashions." Caroline rising with a mild sigh as she pat her bejeweled hair.

"You always dress so extravagantly, I didn't know you had that sort of taste."

"I do what mother thinks is best."

The words gave Arabella pause. She'd always thought her sister adored dressing so loudly, and hadn't considered how much her preferences might have been dictated my their mercurial mother. She turned around on the bench. "Caro... surely you know that you'll find a husband easily, with or without Mama's input in your life."

"I am well aware." The reply was quick, almost dismissive, with Caroline not bothering to turn around as she made her way to the door. "We are going to be late for dinner if we tarry."

Arabella wanted to say more, but they were indeed running late. "Yes, I am coming."

———

Whatever strange mood that had stolen over her sister seemed to have faded by the time they made it downstairs for dinner. Caroline had returned to her demure, smiling self, with half the gentlemen in attendance nearly falling over their feet to give their greetings. At dinner, Arabella found herself seated with Baron Lockhart on her left and Miss Balfour on her right. Caroline, likely due to some matchmaking on the hostess' part, was seated next to Milton. She watched as the two conversed, Caroline enthusing over something or another with a becoming flush as the duke nodded along politely. Again, that obnoxious pit formed in her stomach.

"Your sister and the duke seem to be getting along," Miss Balfour chimed in at her shoulder, shaking Arabella from her silly stupor.

"It seems so," she replied and quickly spooned some of her soup.

"Always so direct, Miss Balfour," Lord Lockhart drawled from her other side.

Miss Balfour scowled. "I don't think I was speaking to you, Lockhart."

"Then do not say such things at dinner."

Arabella looked between the two of them, watching as Miss Balfour narrowed her eyes at Lockhart, who seemed to take great pleasure in needling the woman if his amused smirk was anything to go by. She swallowed another spoonful of soup and cleared her throat. "I hope the rest of your morning was pleasant, Miss Balfour. You seemed quite refreshed from your walk."

"Do call me Cecily. And yes, my morning was lovely, thank you," she said cheerfully, ignoring Lockhart entirely. Arabella heard the baron's scowl at her back.

"I am glad to hear it," she replied, happy to both end whatever standoff was happening between Cecily and Lockhart and take her attention from Milton.

"You must call me Arabella, then. I take it you enjoy morning explorations?"

"It is my favorite time of the day, so quiet and calm. Perfect for a scientific excursion."

Warmth spread in her chest at the thought of meeting a kindred spirit. "I couldn't agree more, regarding the serenity, at least. I'm not much for the natural sciences, though I'm sure the topic is full of fascinations." Her mother had never let her even peek at a single tome containing what she'd deemed 'manly' occupations, lest Arabella be given the death sentence of a bluestocking label. *'You'd become like that pitiful Miss Balfour, twenty-five with no prospects in sight,'* her mother had said with dramatic horror. All the good that policy did, Arabella thought with an inward snort.

"Oh, it is a most fascinating subject, Miss Hughs, and I am happy to find someone who agrees with me on that front." Cecily's eyes all but sparkled. "This estate has been rife with a rich variety of wildlife."

"Here we go," Lord Lockhart muttered under his breath.

Aside from a mild glare in his direction, Cecily ignored him and continued with her impassioned conversation. "I had a wonderful time observing the lake. It is not often I am able to observe things in such a tranquil setting, me being in London more often than not. Mama prefers it, you see." Cecily ended that statement with poorly concealed derision.

"You don't like London, I take it?"

"Despises it, actually," Lord Lockhart chimed in, before continuing with his meal.

Cecily took a sip of wine. "For once, he is correct. Town is far too loud and dirty for me. I much prefer the endless green, fresh air, and *solitude* of the country. But enough about me. How did your sketching go? I noticed you had supplies with you when we crossed paths."

And just when she thought she'd finally driven Milton from her mind, Cecily's innocuous question brought on the image of his stupid face in full force. "Fine," she blurted, her gaze straying across the table once more. Caroline was going on about something that seemed to interest her greatly, her eyes alight with joy as she talked at a rapid pace. Milton nodded along politely, but Arabella couldn't discern anything else from his expression. He darted a glance at her, their eyes meeting for a moment before she looked back at her table-mate, heart hammering. "The lake was beautiful. I may turn the sketch into a full painting upon my return to London."

"How lovely," Cecily replied sincerely. "There are many such beautiful sights about, or at least I was told by Lord Thurmont during the tour he gave me of the house."

There was a choke to her left. Lord Lockhart set down his wine and lightly smacked his chest. "Thurmont took you on a tour?"

Cecily raised an eyebrow. "Yes, and it was lovely. He told me of many interesting areas peppered around the estate. Speaking of which," she turned her attention back to Arabella. "Apparently, the ruins of the original medieval keep are only a half hour's stroll from the house. The foundation and an outer wall are still standing. I was planning to go there tomorrow morning with Mrs. Parson. Would you like to come along? I'm sure it would make for an excellent sketch."

"Mrs. Parson?" The name was unfamiliar.

Cecily leaned closer and discreetly pointed farther down the table. "The lady in grey, next to Miss Russel."

Arabella spotted the infamous heiress, the daughter of a prominent shipping magnate, and then the lady in question. Despite the drab gown she wore, Mrs. Parson was quite the beauty, with sleek dark hair and a delicate face. She was sipping her soup as Miss Russel chatted animatedly, glancing warily about every once in a while. "I see her."

"She's Miss Russel's paid companion. Rumor has it that she was hired to teach her charge proper deportment amongst the Ton. No one knows who she is, however, except that she is a young widow." Considering that Miss Russel's reception into society had been lukewarm at best and downright hostile at worst, as happened with most heiresses of trade, the explanation made sense. Mrs. Parson seemed a peculiar young woman, but if Cecily liked her, then she was surely of good character.

After a moment's consideration, Arabella nodded.

"I would gladly accept your invitation." Anything to keep her mind off Milton.

"Wonderful! I'll look for you in the foyer come dawn."

The two shared a smile before continuing on with their meal. They continued discussing tomorrow's plans, with Lockhart chiming in with some barbed comment or another directed at Cecily, who replied without missing a beat. Arabella found their banter amusing, and it almost distracted her from the distinct sensation of another's eyes on her.

Almost.

———

Nathan took a bracing sip of his wine as the soup course was laid before him, doing his damndest to pay attention to Miss Caroline Hughs and not her sister across from him and further down the table.

"This must be one of the most extravagant house parties I've ever attended," his companion mused as she took a graceful spoonful of soup. The sapphires and diamonds in her hair glittered as she moved, adding to the shine of the diamond parure she wore. It was just a tad too garish, he decided, the overwhelming glow it encased her in more off-putting than alluring.

"Yes, it is quite extravagant," he said absently as his gaze strayed to Miss Hughs once more. She quietly sipped her soup, her flaxen hair styled into a simple chignon and decorated with a single emerald comb matching her green dinner gown. The lady looked positively pretty in a real sort of way that he found far more inviting. She had a mouth made for smiling, and he had the urge to be the one to put the expression on her face. Her eyes lifted, and he quickly averted his gaze lest she catch him staring. Miss Caroline said something, and he turned his attention back to her. "I beg your pardon?"

She smiled patiently. "I asked if you've had a chance to further your acquaintance with my sister. I understand that your first meeting did not go well?"

"I have not, unfortunately," he lied. Every meeting with her had been improper as improper could be, and he certainly would not tell her about that note. Nathan wondered if Miss Hughs had read it yet and what she thought of it. He'd been quite sincere in his apology and hoped she hadn't taken too much offense.

"That's a shame, for she is wonderful company. I'm not sure what I would do without her grounding my more fanciful notions."

Now here was a topic he was interested in. "You are close?"

"As close as sisters can be," she replied. "To be honest, I think she is the only person I truly trust in this world. I wish others could see her finer qualities. Beauty isn't everything, you know."

The statement held not a hint of artifice. He'd have expected her to prop herself up with such wise words, but Miss Caroline seemed to genuinely believe them. A knot formed in his throat. Gregory likely would have spoken similar words. "That is a wonderful bond to have with one's sibling. And I must agree. Your sister is perfectly lovely."

"So you have spoken."

He took a sip of his wine. "Only in passing since the party has started. She apologized for the ball."

"Of course she did. Bella is always magnanimous as long as you give her reason to be." Miss Caroline shook her head. "It is frustrating that the Ton thinks her so bitter, for it is quite the opposite, I assure you."

"I'm beginning to realize that." Guilt speared him anew at his impulsive questioning of her at the lake. It seemed he was even more off the mark regarding her than he had first thought. "The Ton can be a fickle beast."

"Indeed, Your Grace. Oh, but don't pity dear Bella. She has had her share of suitors, even if small. Why, just last year there was a reasonably serious courtship with a viscount." Miss Caroline winced after the words, as if she hadn't meant to utter them.

"What happened?"

"I don't know the particulars," she said quickly and took a sip of her soup. She swallowed heartily. "I only bring it up to prove that Bella has exceptional qualities and would make an excellent companion if given the chance."

Something was odd about the way Miss Caroline spoke on the matter, but Nathan wouldn't pry, curious as he was about this supposed suitor. He cast another glance at Miss Hughs. She was conversing with

Miss Balfour, whilst Lockhart sulked on her other side. Things must be going poorly for the man's bet regarding the bluestocking, for Miss Balfour was just about the only person he knew who could put the baron is such a sour mood. Miss Hughs laughed at something her companion said, the expression lighting up her face in the most extraordinary way. It shouldn't be surprising that someone else might have seen past the Ton's judgement and given her attention. He hoped she hadn't been too disappointed that such a courtship had fallen through. He imagined her listless and heartbroken, that warm face marred by melancholy, and felt a surge of anger on her behalf. Shaking himself from his thoughts, Nathan returned his attention to Miss Caroline. If he spent too long staring at Miss Hughs in the manner that he was, others might take note and assume there was something between them, or that he was interested in her. Which he wasn't beyond a normal curiosity and the fact that he needed her for that mare, not in the least.

"Are you alright, Nathan? You seem distracted," his mother said from his other side.

"Perfectly fine, mother, thank you."

"Good." She darted her eyes toward Miss Caroline, her encouraging look unmistakable. He understood her meaning without her needing to say it, wondering just how much his mother wanted him to consider the lady. That she had been seated next to him, leaving only her and Miss Caroline as conversation partners, made him wonder if she had arranged the seating up with Lady Thurmont. Lady Drummel being seated on Miss Caroline's other side only furthered his suspicions. The older women were certainly tenacious, that was for sure.

Alas, he didn't think it was meant to be. Miss Caroline was a beauty and possessed of a lovely temperament, but he felt not an ounce of interest in her beyond friendship. But that was a conversation to be had in private. For now, he returned his mother's smile and continued conversing with Miss Caroline, doing his damndest not to allow his eyes to stray across the table, even as the melodic laughter of a certain wallflower caressed his ears and demanded attention. He said an inward prayer of thanks when dinner finally ended, the strain of keeping a polite interest in his companion almost too much to bear by the last course.

———

Nathan exhaled a sigh of relief upon entering the drawing room after dinner, though this relief was short-lived as his friends all but descended on him in the corner of the room like a pack of wolves.

"So," Thurmont asked, almost gleeful. "How is your progress?"

Milton rolled his eyes. "So nosy."

"Lockwood's abysmal odds are already obvious," Kirkwood said. "I think we all saw how horrid dinner just was for him."

"You just had to give me Cecily Balfour, didn't

you?" Lockhart replied with a grimace. "Bloody barbarous chit," he muttered into his port.

"Come now," Nathan said with a raised eyebrow. "Surely she isn't that horrible. Miss Hughs seems to like her."

"Paying close attention to your mark, I see," Thurmont said, the suggestive tone in his voice unmistakable.

He felt himself begin to flush but managed to suppress it. "Not really. Just some observations."

"Liar," Kirkwood said, the shrewd marquess not missing a thing. "She wouldn't be staring at you with such moon eyes if you hadn't done something between the ball and now."

Nathan blinked. "Moon eyes?" He laughed heartily, enough that some of the other gentlemen in the room looked their way. After settling his mirth, he continued with a lowered voice. "I'll admit I have interacted with her, but let me assure you that such an expression is the last thing she is doing."

"So, things are going poorly for you as well?" Lockhart looked downright hopeful, as if relieved to have a comrade-in-arms struggling as much as he was.

Nathan thought for a moment. "I... am not sure," he finally admitted.

"Not sure?" Thurmont gave him an incredulous stare. "She's either going to do it or not, Milton. Which is it?"

"It's complicated," he replied, unsure of how to explain the odd air between himself and Miss Hughs.

The men looked at each other, and then back at him, mouths spreading in slow, knowing grins. "Complicated, you say?" Kirkwood said, the suggestion in his tone unmistakable.

Thurmont looked on the verge of laughter. "Do not tell me I've solved your duchess problem?"

"Hush," Nathan snapped back, darting a glance around the room. Thankfully, no one seemed to be paying them much attention anymore. "Don't be ridiculous." Despite his harsh tone, however, the thought wasn't as distressing as he would have imagined, much to his confusion. She was interesting, far more interesting than any of the other debutantes he'd met so far. Would it be so impossible to consider her as a perspective courtship? If she would even speak to him, that was. A busy drawing room with his friends jeering at him wasn't the place to make these considerations, however, and Lockhart's probing stare was not helping matters. "I'm far more concerned about that mare of yours, Thurmont."

"Are you?" The earl replied, playful and doubting in equal measures.

He was saved from having to retort by the ladies entering the room, forcing them all to shut up about the topic. He swallowed as Miss Caroline and her mother made their way towards him, Miss Hughs following just behind.

"Excuse me, gentlemen. I will retire for the evening," he said, ducking from the amused group and making a beeline for the door, being sure to avoid the women heading his way. Several people looked at him curiously as he sedately fled, but they could come to whatever conclusion they wished. His mind was far too jumbled to mingle, even more so under the auspices of an enchanting pair of brown eyes.

Chapter Six

Arabella inhaled the crisp morning air as she made her way down the trail Cecily had talked about last night. She'd waited for the other woman in the foyer for quite some time, only to receive a note from her maid informing her she would be running late and to go on ahead. Deciding that it would give her some time to sketch the ruins, Arabella heeded the advice and went on her way. The sky was cloudy with a refreshing cool summer breeze, and Arabella hugged her arms around her sketchbook as she walked. After a good half hour trek, the ruins came into view. They were indeed impressive, with the stone facade of nearly an entire wall still intact along with the foundation. She stopped to admire the sight, debating on the best angle to begin her sketching. Some movement amongst the stones caught her eye, and her stomach dropped as a familiar man emerged from around a corner.

Milton.

He spotted her almost immediately and raised his hand with a hesitant wave. "We seem to have a knack for running into each other in the mornings."

"It would appear so," she replied, not hiding the suspicion from her voice.

"You don't think I planned this on purpose, do you?"

Arabella clutched her sketchbook closer to her chest. "I wouldn't put it past you."

"It would be quite convenient, I agree. Alas, this is a mere coincidence. Lockhart is the one who invited me." He cast an exasperated look around them. "Though he is nowhere to be found. I don't even know why he wanted to come here so early in the first place. I've never seen the man up earlier than noon."

He seemed sincere enough that she believed him. "That is odd."

Milton shrugged. "He's an odd fellow." There was an awkward pause before he spoke. "Did you get my note?"

It was the first time they'd spoken since that episode at the lake, she realized, and after receiving his missive. "Yes," she began tentatively, unsure of how to respond. "I appreciate it and the flower."

"You seemed like a lavender kind of lady. I am glad."

She rose an eyebrow. "A lavender kind of lady?"

"Subtle, often overlooked, but really quite lovely when one bothers to pay them any mind."

It was a glorious, perfectly executed compliment that did its intended job. She could already feel the butterflies swarming in her belly and had to remind herself of the man's previous duplicity in order to stay them. "You seem to have quite the interest in flowers, Your Grace."

"Oh, not in the slightest, outside of the normal appreciation for their beauty. Kirkwood, however, would disagree, and I've heard many a lecture on the minutiae of one obscure bloom or other from him. I know far more than I care to, but the man gets so enthused that none of us have the heart to stop him from going on about it."

The Marquess of Kirkwood was a known avid botanist, and many often wondered just why the quiet man was part of Milton's rowdy set, her included. "Never?"

He shrugged. "That's part of being a friend. Surely you do the same with your own lady friends." When she didn't answer, Milton tilted his head, the casual smile slipping from his face. "You have friends, yes?"

"Of course," she replied quickly, a hot flush of embarrassment creeping up her cheeks.

But Milton seemed unconvinced, crossing his arms and raising a dark eyebrow. "Oh?"

"Yes," she replied, putting on an unjustified air of indignation to mask her embarrassed panic. Arabella had never been the best at socializing and had struggled to form any close attachments during her debut. Once Caroline had her come-out and those rumors had begun to circulate, any slim possibility of outside companionship had faded. Her recalcitrance during that second season certainly didn't help matters. "My sister and I are quite close, in spite of what the rumors may say and you might think. And I am here to meet Miss Balfour for a pleasant morning of assessing the ruins."

Milton's eyes softened on her form. "I am sorry for my words concerning your sister yesterday."

Eager to latch on to this new topic and not dwell on her lack of friends, Arabella nodded. "Thank you, though I was willing to accept your note as an apology."

"I am glad to clear the air. I get heated when discussion of siblings comes up, and bad blood between family members bothers me considerably enough to cloud my judgment." There was a pain in his eyes that she'd never seen before, and she wondered if he was referring to the family tragedy. Arabella knew little of the carriage accident that had claimed the late duke and his eldest son ten years ago, only that it had damaged the wife and son left behind deeply and was the apparent cause of the duchess' social seclusion.

"It is alright. I understand," she replied. An awkwardness settled between them, the silence painful enough that she almost wished to return to the discussion of her friendless state. Milton's visage grew distant, and she grasped for a way to dispel the sudden pal settling over them. She cleared her throat. "In exchange for your second apology," she watched as his eyes lit up once more, "I have decided to believe your fanciful excuse for coming to these ruins so early in the morning and conveniently at the same time as I."

"Drat," he scoffed, slapping his hat on the side of this thigh. "I thought you were about to say you'd give me that waltz after all." The smile told her he wasn't serious . "Ah well. A lad can dream, I suppose."

She laughed. "I'm afraid you are still unforgiven on that front, Your Grace. It'll take a lot more than a pretty note and some kind words get me to help with that ridiculous wager."

"I didn't do that for the wager." His voice was low, so low she almost didn't hear it over the breeze whistling through the ruins. He pushed off the wall and was in front of her in three long strides, so close she could smell the faint scent of his cologne. "I did it because you are a lovely person who didn't deserve to be offended by my stupid words."

Arabella swallowed, heart hammering in her chest as she processed the statement. But then, she reminded herself, he'd used pretty words on her before. There was no reason to trust him, even if his eyes seemed to envelop her with dark, intense sincerity. Was it her, or was he a step closer than before? "I don't believe you," she charged, her voice barely a whisper over the morning breeze.

"Believe this, then," he muttered back, ducking his head and taking her lips before she could even form a coherent thought.

—————

This was, possibly, the most foolish thing he had done in a long time, Nathan mused as he lowered his head to kiss Miss Hughs in the middle of a ruined castle where Lockhart and Miss Balfour might come upon them at any moment. Half of him hoped she might shove him away and thwart this impulsive move, but Miss Hughs stayed firmly planted in place as his mouth landed on hers. What had compelled him, Nathan did not know. Perhaps his frustrations at her refusal to believe him, or even seeing those ruby red lips curl so enticingly as she sneered at his attempted overtures, had played a role, but the reason hardly mattered now. A shiver stole through him at the feel of her soft lips, a slither of heat that snaked its way down his spine and thrummed in his blood. Goodness, they weren't even kissing properly, and he was this riled up. He needed to stop before things got out of hand. But all reason fled when Miss Hughs touched her palm to his chest and, rather than shove as he'd expected, leaned further into him. Nathan cupped her face in his hand and slanted his mouth to fit more snugly against her lips. Her palm pushed more, fingers curling into his waistcoat and searing the skin beneath. Her nails dug into his chest and the sensation was enough to jar him back into sense. He pulled himself away with a sudden lurch and took two large steps back, at a loss for words to explain what the hell he had just done.

Miss Hughs remained in place, taking him in with

wide eyes. She held a hand to her chest, her breath coming in quick bursts. "Your Grace..."

He winced at the title. Somehow, after what had just transpired, it sounded wrong coming from her lips. "Milton, please."

"Milton," she corrected and then fell silent. Her eyes roved everywhere but over him, her hand still clutching the loose ribbons of her bonnet to her chest.

Feeling like twice the cad, he held out a hand. "Miss Hughs, I—"

"Arabella?" a familiar voice called from the other side of the ruins. "Are you here?"

Miss Hughs took a visible swallow, inhaling before calling in a calm, clear voice. "One moment, Cecily. I am coming." She returned her attention to him, all traces of earlier distress replaced by irritation. "You need to go," she mouthed. Grassy footsteps grew closer, Miss Balfour's voice mingling with that of another woman's over the wind.

The situation was dire, and Nathan could only nod and hurry away from the scene. He ducked behind a wall just as Miss Balfour and the other woman emerged from the other side. Miss Hughs conversed with them, her voice calm, as if the explosive scene a mere minute ago hadn't happened. Nathan could only hope that the two women hadn't seen Highwind tied to a nearby tree. Lockhart would not show, that much was obvious if he was this late. The idiot had likely overslept and forgotten.

It wasn't until he'd mounted Highwind and was

well on his way back to the manor that the frantic energy thrumming through him abated enough to allow Nathan to relax. With the excitement of the kiss and their near discovery finally waning, he was able to take a moment to think things rationally. His attraction to Miss Hughs was no surprise. He just hadn't expected it to hit him with such force after having only known her for a few days. When that initial interest had turned into pure lust, he had no idea, but the reality could not be denied. The real question was whether to do anything about it.

He thought for a moment, envisioned embarking on a proper courtship. Her lack of respect for his title was refreshing, her forthright nature putting him at ease. There was nothing contrived in their interactions, no games being played beneath the surface conversation. Her family was respectable, her understated beauty undeniable, and their mothers were old friends. He was certain the concerning rumors about her were false. Everything lined up, and there was no reason not to consider her.

Except for one, of course.

The fuzzy warmth that had been sneaking through him as he listed all the reasons to court Miss Hughs fizzled away as he remembered her face after their kiss. He'd distressed her, disgusted her, and more than likely offended her, making it clear that his advances were not only ill-warranted, but entirely unwanted. Before, he'd thought she might feel a sliver of attraction for him. She watched him so much and became so flustered around his person that he couldn't think of any other reason. But, perhaps he'd imagine things and his own feelings had tricked him into seeing this odd bond forming between them. No, it made far more sense that Miss Hughs wanted nothing to do with him, and why would she? He was using her in a bet to win a bloody horse, after all.

For the first time since beginning this whole adventure, the callousness of the bet hit him. It seemed so harmless in the beginning but, thinking on it, the potential for hurt was obvious. He slowed Highwind to a walk as the house loomed and eyed the approaching stables with a sinking stomach. Since when had he allowed his moral character to be compromised over something as frivolous as a racehorse?

"I'm being a bastard, aren't I?" He said with a pat on Highwind's neck. The horse only snorted in reply, as if agreeing with the sentiment. The stallion was extra grumpy with his hay once Nathan put him away, and it was amusing enough to cheer him from his souring mood. Perhaps Miss Hughs and Bellona were both a lost cause, but he wouldn't despair. There were plenty of young ladies out there he had yet to meet. Surely one of them would stir him in the same way as Miss Hughs had. He just needed to apply himself more rigorously to the search. Feeling optimistic, Nathan headed into the house. A destination in mind, he made a beeline for the stairs and passed his chambers. He stopped in front of a door further down the hall and rapped on the wood with a polite knock. A muted grumble answered the question of Lockhart's location this morning. Upon opening the door, Nathan found the baron sprawled on the bed, still wearing his evening clothes from the previous night. "Good God, man. Tell me you didn't get foxed all by yourself last night?"

Lockhart cracked open one shadowed eye. "That you, Milton?" He sat up on his elbows with a bleary scan of the room. "Oh, hell. Is it morning already? I must have fallen asleep."

"Drinking into oblivion might not be out of character, but surely even you wouldn't do such at a respectable house party." Nathan sat on the edge of the bed and gave Lockhart's shin a light punch. "We had an appointment, you dunderhead. I waited like an idiot for nearly an hour up at those ruins." And had an explosive rendezvous with Miss Hughs. But Nathan wasn't quite ready to share that tidbit with anyone, if ever.

Lockhart yawned and sat up fully. "I wasn't drinking. I was thinking."

"About?"

"Nothing, really."

"Nothing kept you up all evening to the point of sleeping in your dinner clothes?"

Lockhart must have sensed the concern in Nathan's tone, for he waved a dismissive hand in response. "I'm fine. It's a silly matter, really." He stretched. "Did you run into the ladies at the ruins?"

Nathan frowned. "How did you know they would be there?" He recalled last night's dinner where Miss Hughs and Miss Balfour chatted whilst Lockhart sulked to the side. A thought struck him. "You over-heard their plans last night."

"I had hoped to spend some time with Miss Balfour and thought the presence of others would shield me from her venom."

"What happened to make her hate you so?"

Lockhart shrugged. "She hates everything I stand for and thinks of me as a stain on her perfect, moral little world."

There was a bite to the baron's words that told him there was more to the story, but Nathan knew when not to pry. He wondered if last night's contemplations had anything to do with the woman. "You seem to have the hardest task out of all of us."

"And don't I know it." Lockhart hauled his legs over the side. "Speaking of which, how goes your task?"

He was seconds away from informing him of his intention to quit but paused. He had nearly half the season to perform the dare, and Thurmont no doubt had some horrifying idea in mind to punish him were he to fail. It wouldn't hurt to delay the inevitable and neglect to share his decision until the very end. "It's going," was all he said.

"Well, you'll have ample time to talk to her today. Lady Thurmont has many activities planned."

Outside of an eventual apology for his untoward behavior, talking to Miss Arabella Hughs would be the last thing he did for the rest of the party, and he had the distinct feeling such actions would please her immensely.

Chapter Seven

Arabella huffed in her chair as she stared out at the lawns from her bedroom window. Most of the houseguests were milling about outside, preparing for the afternoon of outdoor games that Lady Thurston had arranged. Yet again, she found herself holed up in her room in a desperate bid to avoid Milton. She raised a finger to her lips, the memory of the kiss yesterday morning still fresh on her mind. It had been such an impulsive thing to do, and with Milton, of all people. Yet, despite the disgust Arabella wanted to feel, only warmth skittered up her spine and settled in her belly at the thought of doing so again. Which would never happen, of course. She would never allow it, and if Milton's behavior for the rest of that day was any indication, then he wouldn't allow it, either.

After an admittedly lovely morning with Cecily and Mrs. Parsons exploring the ruins and sketching the crumbling ancient walls, Arabella had nearly forgotten about her explosive encounter with Milton. Cecily had turned out to be a wonderful companion, full of thoughtful and entertaining knowledge about the old pile that she'd apparently read about in Thurston's expansive library, whilst Mrs. Parsons carried on with a surprising level of wit and elegance for a lady of her class. By luncheon, Arabella had been in a much better mood, even as the specter of the kiss returned full force upon their return to the house. She'd fully intended to locate Milton and talk things out. No doubt the emotional conversation they'd shared and the idyllic location had addled their senses, for surely the man wasn't so much of a cad as to pretend an infatuation for her just to get his hands on that horse.

No, they'd have talked things out, apologized, and promised never to do so again, as was proper. At least, that had been the plan until it became quite apparent that Milton wanted nothing to do with her. Every time she'd walked towards him, even subtly, he'd slipped away in the opposite direction with one excuse or another. Whether it was requiring a drink or miraculously spotting one of his friends who had been in the room for the entire time as he, Milton had slipped away from her before any polite conversation could turn into an attempt to clear the air between them. While, thankfully, his behavior was subtle enough that the rest of the guests hadn't caught on, it was more than obvious to Arabella that she was being avoided. That he had no qualms with spending time with either her mother or sister only confirmed her suspicions.

While indeed the kiss had been shocking, surely he hadn't found her as unattractive as all that? Right?

While she disliked him, that he'd found the contact so appalling was a bit of a blow to her feminine pride. She'd imagined any woman might feel hurt at such a reaction from a man she'd kissed, even if said kiss was unwanted. Unable to withstand the embarrassment, Arabella now sulked in her room, hoping to avoid the planned game. She narrowed her eyes as guests spilled out onto the lawn, Milton among them. Caroline was at his right, the pair once again making a pretty sight. Perhaps it was for the best that she avoid him, for if Caroline's initial interest ever turned into a full infatuation, she did not want to be there to see it or get in the way. Turning away from the sight with a scowl, she thought about what to do with the rest of the day before a knock on the door interrupted her thoughts.

"Arabella? Might I speak to you?" Cecily spoke from the other side.

"Come in," she replied, her mood brightening at seeing her newfound friend. Cecily slid inside and quietly shut the door behind her, dressed smartly in a pale green walking set. Despite her bluestocking tendencies, Arabella noticed that the woman seemed to enjoy fashion.

"Are you not going to play?" Cecily asked with a tilt of her head. "I thought you liked the outdoors."

"I do. I just..." She scrambled for a reason to explain herself that didn't involve sharing the kiss. "I'm not in the mood."

"Drat," Cecily mumbled to herself, before smiling. "Ah, well. I hope you feel better."

"Is everything alright?"

"Yes," she assured, before frowning. "Well, no. I was hoping to enlist your help, but don't worry about it. It is a minor annoyance, really." She crossed her arms and glared at the floor. "The game is to be played in pairs, and Lockhart has been pestering me to partner up."

"Why ever for? You two seem to despise one another, if you don't mind my frankness."

Cecily threw her hands in the air. "I do not know, but the man has been following me around since luncheon claiming that all the other ladies wouldn't partner with him, which I know to be a ridiculous lie, and my mother is encouraging it! I thought to ask you to partner with him, otherwise I'll make a supreme ass of myself in front of everyone."

Arabella smothered a laugh. "I'd rather you not do that." She looked out the window once more. Several couples had already paired up, though Caroline seemed to have left the duke and was nowhere to be found. She spied Lord Thurmont next to Miss Russel, whom was chatting his ear off whilst the earl himself appeared to want to be anywhere but where he was. Mrs. Parsons stood to the side with some others who weren't playing and was looking anxiously at the couple, no doubt worried that Miss Russel would act improper, which was entirely possible if Thurmont's almost pained expression as the poor girl prattled on were any sign. Milton and Lockhart were together in the middle of the lawn, the latter glancing about him every few seconds, likely searching for poor Cecily whilst the former appeared to tease him. "I'll partner with Lockhart if you take His Grace."

"You've decided to come after all?" Cecily's eyes lit up with relieved hope.

"Yes." Why should she hide away when Milton was the one who'd misbehaved? She wasn't so much of a coward to let a mere single man affect her so. She'd had enough of that last year.

"It's a deal, then."

After quickly changing, Arabella followed Cecily down to the lawns.

"Oh, one more thing," her companion said before they exited the house. "I was planning on another activity tonight, and I've enlisted a few other ladies to come along. Would you care to join us?"

It was on the tip of her tongue to politely decline the invitation, but then Milton's shocked face as he'd questioned her lack of friends came into infuriating view. Perhaps it would be a good idea to socialize a bit more. "Very well," she said.

"Excellent, meet me in my room after dinner," Cecily replied as they emerged onto the sun soaked lawn. Lockhart perked up upon spotting them and trotted over, Milton following behind at a sedate pace and eying her warily.

"There you are, Miss Balfour," Lockhart said with

a near saccharine sweetness that did not come close to reaching his eyes.

"Yes, here I am." Cecily's smile was so tight, Arabella half expected her jaw to twitch from the strain. She gestured to Arabella. "And I've brought a straggler along."

"Miss Hughs. A pleasure to talk again after such a *pleasant* dinner." Though the baron was ostensibly speaking to her, his eyes were on Cecily like a pair of daggers.

"Miss Hughs," Milton greeted with a tight nod.

"Your Grace." She smiled cordially, looking at him with a straightforward gaze before turning her attention squarely towards Lockhart. "Miss Balfour tells me you are in want of a partner, My Lord." Out of the corner of her eye she saw Milton shift and darted a quick glance at him. His mouth formed a thin line, eyes narrowing. She tried not to widen her smile. Let's see how he liked being ignored for once. "Might I volunteer for the task?"

"Do not say I never look out for you, dear neighbor," Cecily said, her tight smile turning victorious.

"I did not realize you two were neighbors," Arabella noted with curiosity.

"Oh, yes," Lockhart replied, smooth as ever, despite the ice in his eyes as he looked upon Cecily. "Our families have existed side by side for several generations. I remember fondly the days your child self would follow me around like a little puppy dog, Miss Balfour."

Cecily flushed, and Arabella feared what she might say next to rile the situation up even further. Blessedly, Milton cut in between them. "The game is beginning, I believe. Miss Balfour, would you do me the honor of being my partner? I'm a terrible shot."

"Shall we, Lord Lockhart?" Arabella said with a beaming smile at the scowling baron. She could still feel Milton's eyes on her, despite him walking off with Miss Balfour. He wouldn't get the satisfaction of her attention, and the thought of her slight irritating him was gratifying to the extreme.

Lord Lockhart wiped all traces of aggression from his face as he turned away from the pair, his relaxed air returning. "Of course, Miss Hughs. Lead the way."

"I'm afraid I don't know the rules, My Lord." She hadn't played a game of bowls in her life, having been invited to no house parties and being part of a family that spent little time together outside of the social requirements. She tried to imagine her frigid father tossing around a lawn ball and nearly laughed aloud.

"That's alright," Lord Lockhart replied, his eyes straying back to the duke and Cecily and narrowing.

Arabella blinked, watching him tense as the pair chatted. "Are you... jealous?" She clamped her hand over her mouth. "I said that aloud, didn't I?"

Lockhart laughed, long, rich, and so loud that the others on the lawn were staring at him. "I'm not sure what is more amusing," he said after calming down, "that slip up or the fact that you think I care at all what

Miss Balfour does. Come along, I'll show you how to throw the ball properly."

Arabella followed him up the lawn, noting that he made it a point not to look anywhere near Milton and Cecily. She did the same, knowing that it would irritate Milton even more. Served him right.

———

"They seem to be getting along, though I suppose Lockhart gets on well with just about everyone when he puts his mind to it."

Nathan tore his gaze away from Arabella and Lockhart to look at his companion. He'd partnered with her in a panic, hoping that separating the two might diffuse what was fast becoming a scene. No doubt Lockhart was irritated with him for taking away his quarry. "That he does, Miss Balfour. Though, from what he's told me, that same affability does not extend to you." Lockhart made no secret of his disdain for the famous bluestocking, despite their families being neighbors for a good several generations. Nathan could vaguely remember the two getting along during the handful of times he'd visited between terms, the little girl following Lockhart around like a besotted puppy. Something seemed to have changed in the proceeding years, though his friend never cared to share what.

Miss Balfour let out a rather unladylike snort that would have had most mamas reeling. "He drives me up the wall, if you must know."

"And yet I cannot help but notice your gaze straying to his person on more than one occasion." Several times he'd seen Miss Balfour casting discreet glances the baron's way whenever the man wasn't looking, making Nathan wonder just how true her animosity was.

She raised a cool eyebrow, though the disinterested effect was diminished somewhat by the red blush creeping across her cheeks. "Just like you keep doing the same to Miss Hughs?"

Now it was his turn to flush. "Touche, Miss Balfour."

"I think she likes you too, for what it's worth."

He coughed into his hand. "Hardly."

She shrugged. "We will have to agree to disagree, Your Grace. I am an excellent judge of character."

"Except when it comes to Lord Lockhart," he replied pointedly.

"Back to that tiresome subject again?" A giggle sounded, and Nathan watched Miss Balfour glare at Lockhart in thinly disguised disdain as he playfully demonstrated the proper throwing technique to Miss Hughs, who seemed quite amused with the baron's charming instruction. "He's frivolous to an appalling degree."

"I suppose. Though, such things aren't always a sign of villainy, despite what you seem to think," he replied calmly, feeling the need to defend his friend. Yes, Lockhart was the flightiest and rowdiest of their group, but he was also the most loyal friend he'd ever known. When Nathan had been a sobbing mess after the tragedy, Lockhart had been the one to spend immeasurable hours patting his back and murmuring words of comfort as he cried like a child in his new study, had been Lockhart who'd walked with him to his seat at parliament whilst he'd inwardly cringed with nerves, and it had been Lockhart who'd viciously led the charge to eviscerate any petty gossips who'd dared invent some lurid reasonings for his mother's absence from society. It was for these reasons why, unlike Miss Balfour's thinly disguised distress at watching Lockhart charm another woman, Nathan didn't feel threatened in the least by his casual flirtations with Miss Hughs, merely a spark of envy that he himself wasn't the one in Lockhart's place. He tried to imagine Miss Hughs chuckling at his own attempts to flirt in a similar matter and failed miserably. No doubt she'd scowl and humiliate him again, especially after that bloody kiss. He swallowed the wave of arousal at the memory of her soft lips and the charming way she'd clutched his chest as he'd deepened it. That such a mild kiss could send him so out of sorts was embarrassing to the supreme and was a testament to this unfathomable attraction, one entirely undesired in light of the obvious fact that she wanted nothing to do with him.

"We will have to agree to disagree, Your Grace," Miss Balfour said with a sniff, knocking him from his deteriorating thoughts.

He tore his gaze from Miss Hughs. "Very well," he replied, not wanting to direct any of her ire at him.

That she could terrify the normally unflappable Lockhart to such a degree meant she was quite formidable, and he already had one difficult lady to handle. His ears prickled as Miss Hughs giggled again, and it took everything he had not to look and see what Lockhart was doing to illicit such a reaction. No doubt his friend was getting his revenge and trying to needle Nathan, and Miss Hughs seemed determined to aid him in that endeavor. Was she angry at him for avoiding her? The possibility confused him, for he'd thought that was precisely what she would have wanted.

'I think she likes you too, for what it's worth.' He rolled Miss Balfour's words around in his mind, debating their accuracy for a moment before shaking his head. Preposterous. The woman had made her dislike of him clear. Even if it had felt like she wanted to return his kiss in the morning. Again, he remembered her soft sigh and the way she'd clutched him before he'd wrenched away. He dared another glance, only to see her still chatting with Lockhart and paying him no mind. No, not a chance.

"Everyone!" Lady Thurmont's voice called over the green. She stood at the top of the terrace, holding the white ball in her hands. The other non-players mingled about just behind. His mother and Lady Drummel were conversing, the latter appearing a tad morose, likely due to the fact that Miss Caroline had bowed out of the game. He'd have to tell his mother soon that he'd knocked Miss Caroline off the list. Said lady was off to one side, staring at her sister and Lockhart with an obvious note of irritation. Did she have her cap set for Lockhart, perhaps, and was jealous of Miss Hughs? It seemed unlikely. From what little he'd observed of Miss Caroline, she hadn't seemed to favor any gentleman beyond a passing conversation, himself included. Before he could think further on the matter, Lady Thurmont cleared her throat. "Since you all have found your pairs, let us begin our game. The rules are the same as a normal match, except that only the closest ball to the target out of the two of you will be counted. Thurmont," she called to her son, holding up the ball. "Will you do the honors?"

Nathan looked at his friend with pity. The poor man had somehow wound up with Miss Georgiana Russel as his partner. Heiress to a successful shipping company with a father who'd recently acquired a baronetcy through dubious means, the lady was a new addition to the Ton and had made a fool of herself at just about every event she could with her lack of manners, likely the reason for the paid companion that was with her. She'd been following Thurmont about for most of the house party, her intentions obvious. Unfortunately for the poor girl, the earl was decidedly not interested. An idea formed in Nathan's head as he watched Thurmont eagerly extricate himself from his companion, something that could be the perfect revenge for starting this entire scheme in the first place. The man did say that the others would get to choose his partner when the time came around. But no,

Nathan decided, he would win far too quickly due to Miss Russel's like of him. Besides, it would be cruel for Thurmont to dance with the lady and get her hopes up.

Watching the earl walking to his mother, Nathan's eyes involuntarily passed over Lockhart and Miss Hughs once more. Lockhart whispered something in her ear, perhaps some commentary on Thurmont's unfortunate situation, and Miss Hughs' lips crunched in suppressed laughter. And then her gaze lifted, her eyes meeting Nathan's. The smile fell from her face, and yet her eyes remained on him. His heart thundered at the contact, those brown eyes fathomless and drawing him in much the same way as the ball.

"I hope I haven't missed much," a playful, accented voice drawled from the terrace, just behind the other onlookers.

"Your Highness," Lady Thurmont gasped, turning sharply and revealing the man at the doorway.

Still in his traveling clothes and flanked by two guards, Prince Derrick of Warcia, Derry to his friends, gave their hostess an apologetic smile. "Apologies for arriving so late, Countess. There was a delay on the way here."

"You are welcome to come and go as you wish, Your Highness," Lady Thurmont replied, her eyes shining with glee. No doubt having an entire prince attending her party was the coup of the season.

"Perhaps we should delay the game, mother, so

that we may see His Highness settled?" Thurmont supplied hopefully.

"I don't wish to impose," Derry replied magnanimously.

But Thurmont's obvious wish to prevent the game overruled. "Nonsense, friend. Come with me, and I'll see you settled."

"I suppose I should go along," Nathan mused.

Miss Balfour cast a baleful glance around the green. "The game is lost, regardless. Everyone is far too excited to concentrate."

"Excuse me," he said with a polite nod. Lockhart had left Miss Hughs and was already making his way towards Thurmont and Derry. The tension that lifted from Nathan upon the baron leaving her company was both relieving and maddeningly perplexing.

CHAPTER EIGHT

ARABELLA KNOCKED on the door to Cecily's room, taking a deep breath to calm her nerves.

"She's here," Cecily's excited voice sounded from within. The door opened, the smiling woman standing behind it. "I'm so glad you decided to join us. Come in!"

Arabella followed her into the room. Miss Russel and Mrs. Parson sat near the window, both women giving her a welcoming smile. Another girl she didn't recognize sat at the foot of Cecily's bed. A pretty woman with flaxen hair and friendly eyes, the stranger seemed charming enough, though her walking dress was a few years out of date.

"This is Miss Jane Lambert," Cecily said. "She's the daughter of a neighboring gentleman, or so she tells me. I met her in the village on my way up a few days ago, and we had a lovely conversation."

"A pleasure," Miss Lambert said, rising a moment

to take a brief curtsey. "My mother is good friends with the family, and Lady Thurmont was kind enough to extend us an invitation to her party. I was delayed at home and only just arrived."

"You've met Mrs. Parson, of course," Cecily said. The companion gave Arabella an elegant nod.

"And you are Miss Russel, though we have not met directly," Arabella said to the other woman.

Miss Russel beamed. "That would be me. Theo told me about her trip with you to the ruins morning, and I was very jealous."

"She insisted on coming along tonight," Mrs. Parson said, a touch of affectionate exasperation in her voice.

"Can't let you have all the fun, now can I?" Miss Russel replied, her refined tones slipping into more common speech.

Mrs. Parson winced. "Your accent, dearest."

Miss Russel blushed with a sheepish smile as if this were a common occurrence. It likely was, if Mrs. Parsons had been employed to such an extensive degree. "Right, apologies."

Cecily smiled. "We don't mind, do we?"

Arabella gave a friendly nod, and Miss Lambert mirrored it. "No trouble, dear." She had no right to judge Miss Russel's failing but admirable attempts to fit in when her own standing amongst society was so abysmal. Miss Russel could be as pretty and charming as she wanted, and the Ton would still shun her. Arabella was spared from that, at least.

"Thank you," Miss Russel replied, her refined accent melting back into place as if she'd never slipped. "So, what exactly is your plan, Miss Balfour?"

"I read something in the library," Cecily replied, excitement shining in her eyes. "I found a travelogue that mentioned this estate, particularly the lake. Apparently, when conditions are just right, the water is so still that you can see the reflection of the entire night sky. The effect is simply devastating during a full moon, supposedly." She pointed to the window. "And as you can see, there is one now. The air is still, so I think we have an excellent shot at seeing this magical effect tonight."

"I've heard similar rumors about the lake in the village," Miss Lambert said. "Why did you not ask Lord Thurmont or his mother about it, Miss Balfour?"

"And tip them off to our plans? You realize this is risky for us to do."

A group of ladies going off on their own in the middle of the night was indeed a mildly scandalous thing, hence why she hadn't brought Caroline along for this little excursion in spite of the woman's protests. "So long as we are careful, it should be alright," Arabella mused. Besides, it wasn't as if she cared much for her reputation any longer, and she supposed the others didn't either if they were here.

As if mirroring her thoughts, Miss Russel shrugged. "Will anyone care about a bunch of nobodies like us?"

"Your father will," Mrs. Parson's replied sternly.

Miss Russel waved a dismissive hand. "Father isn't here. Besides, I'll just tell him I forced you along, and you'll be spared from blame."

"Any objections, Miss Lambert?" Cecily said.

Miss Lambert shook her head. "No, I am alright."

Cecily clapped her hands. "It's settled, then. Let us wait another few hours and be off."

"Very well," Arabella replied, trepidation creeping in despite her enthusiasm. She had the odd feeling that something was going to happen tonight thanks to this impulsive decision, but it was far too late to turn back now.

───────

The air was indeed as still as Cecily claimed when they finally emerged from the kitchen doors onto the expansive lawn, and Arabella inhaled the crisp, sweet summer air. She felt more invigorated than she had in a long while, perhaps owing to the clandestine nature of this trek. The five of them shuffled down the path with only the light of the full moon to light the way. Arabella walked beside Cecily, the others falling behind in muted but excited conversation.

"I never did ask you about the ruins," Cecily murmured.

"Ask me what?"

"I saw someone's horse tied to a tree on our way up. Did you see anyone else? I had worried that Lockhart had shown up to make himself a pest, but that didn't seem to be the case."

While Cecily may have proven herself to be a potential friend, Arabella did not know her well enough to deduce whether she could be trusted with information that put her reputation in jeopardy. Even Caroline didn't know about the kiss yet. "No," she answered, keeping her voice even. "We must have just missed them, whoever they were."

Even in the dim light of the moon, Cecily's doubtful expression was visible. "If you say so."

"Oh, my! It's beautiful," Miss Russel's delighted exclamation cut through the tranquility as they crested a hill. The excitement was well warranted, for the sight that lay before Arabella was truly breathtaking. The waters of the lake were still, as if a mirror had been constructed over the entire length of it, and the vibrant reflection of the shining moon and twinkling stars on the surface made for a fantastical scene straight out of a dream. Cecily and the others gleefully trotted down the path, vocalizing their awe. Even the placid Mrs. Parson couldn't help but to laugh along with the others as they frolicked to the shores. Arabella stayed behind a moment longer, wanting to commit the awe-inspiring scene to memory. Her painting skills wouldn't do the scene justice, but she would damn well try her best.

"Come on, Arabella!" Cecily called from the shore.

"One moment." She looked behind her at the distant facade of the house, wondering if the moon

was bright enough to go back for her sketchbook, and
then froze. A man was walking up the path, nearly to
the base of the hill. Arabella looked at the frolicking
ladies. The tall hill hid them from view, so long as no
one reached its crest as the man was currently about to
do. Alarmed at potential discovery, Arabella frantically
scoured her brain for a solution. Every second she took
to think, the man grew closer, until she was able to
faintly make out his features in the dim light of the
moon. Her heart hammered in her ears, mouth going
dry. "Milton."

He stopped at the foot of the hill, looking almost
startled to see her there. "Miss Hughs?"

"Hush," she snapped in a muted whisper, putting
a finger to her lips for emphasis, as if he could even see
the finer details of her face. She could barely make out
his own in the dim light, but the angular plains she
could make out and his tall, commanding stature were
long familiar to her. "I am not alone."

"No?" There was a hard edge to his voice, as if the
words distressed him.

Gathering the meaning of such a tone, Arabella
almost rolled her eyes. "I am with some new friends."
Punctuating the statement was splash and a girlish
sheik, followed by muffled giggles as whomever had
made the noise was playfully silenced.

He shifted from one foot to the other, silent for a
few awkward moments, before speaking once more in
a far quieter voice. "I will leave you ladies to it, then.
You were here first, after all." His head shifted, and she

imagined he was smiling. "Rest assured, my lips are sealed regarding this late night excursion. Heaven knows how many times the boys and I have done the same."

"Thank you," she whispered back, relief coursing through her at Milton's magnanimity. She shouldn't have been surprised, considering how much of his relaxed personality he showed her.

He rose his hand with a friendly wave. "Goodbye, then."

Some strange sort of panic seized her. This might be the only time they were alone together, considering how determined he was to carve out distance between them. She watched his back fading into the night, her indecision worsening with each step he took.

"You coming, or what?" Cecily shouted playfully, even as the others shushed her.

Arabella put a hand to her chest to stay her thundering heart and wondered if what she was about to do was wise. She turned back to the women. Miss Russel and Cecily had taken their shoes and stockings off and were wading around the shallows, skirts bunched in their hands, whilst Mrs. Pearson lounged with Miss Lambert on the shore. "I've come down with a bit of a headache. I think I may retire, after all."

"If you are sure," Cecily said, her voice tinged with uncertainty.

"Feel better," Miss Russel called.

Mrs. Pearson put a hand to her head. "Between the

two of you, we'll be discovered in no time at all. They already had, not that Arabella would tell them of it.

"Goodnight, everyone," she replied, being sure not to raise her voice too high. The others each waved in reply. Arabella waited until she was out of their site before picking up her pace down the dark path, hoping that Milton hadn't gotten too far.

———

Nathan cursed under his breath as his shot went awry, sending the balls in the exact opposite direction he'd intended.

"I haven't seen you play this badly since Eaton, Milton," Derry drawled, moving to take his own shot. The prince took aim and executed a perfect spin on the ball, as expected. Nathan couldn't count how many times they'd all been thoroughly trounced by the man.

The excitement of the afternoon had given way to evening. Dinner had been a loud affair, Derry's newfound presence taking the attention of just about every houseguest. He himself had been seated at the prince's elbow, and Nathan had used the distraction of his friend's presence to keep from staring at Miss Hughs in the same ridiculous manner he had only a day before.

"He's got a lot on his mind," Thurmont chimed in cheerily. "That horse won't win itself, you know."

"Ah, yes. That silly bet of yours. Kirkwood told me about it. It's Milton and Lockhart first, I hear."

"Don't remind me," Lockhart grumbled, sinking into the armchair he sat in and taking a long swallow of whiskey. The baron had been unusually grumpy after the afternoon's activities, and Nathan wondered if it had anything to do with the hushed and obviously heated exchange he'd seen him have with Miss Balfour on the way back inside. Kirkwood looked up from whatever notes he had been scribbling from his seat on an adjacent sofa and gave Lockhart a lopsided smile. "Doing poorly, as expected."

"We'll see if you have that stupid grin once Thurmont picks out your own difficult chit," Lockhart snapped back.

"Why are you so late, Derry? Wander off again?" Nathan asked, steering the conversation to a safer topic before things got too aggressive thanks to Lockhart's sour mood.

"In a way, yes," he replied, and Nathan nearly rolled his eyes at the cryptic words. Derrick could be a coy bastard at times. He supposed it was natural for a prince to behave as such, as frustrating as it was for the rest of them.

"Get distracted by some fancy piece?" Thurmont inquired with a waggle of his eyebrows.

"Must everything be so lewd with you?" Derry scowled.

"You did not answer the question," Kirkwood noted with a small smirk.

"A ship passing in the night, nothing more, nothing less," he replied before adding with a grumble,

"Bloody nosy bastards. This silly wager of yours is far more interesting than my affairs."

"Will you take part?" Nathan asked. It would be amusing to see the normally placid man flounder around. It was a rare time that Derry was thrown out of sorts.

Alas, it seemed the prince was determined to disappoint them once again this evening, as he gave them a small shake of his head. "I will not."

"Is there nothing we can tempt you with? There are some extravagant rewards on the line," Thurmont said. "Milton here is getting that damn horse he's been begging me about for the past year." He wasn't, but Nathan wouldn't be sharing that for quite some time for the sake of his dignity.

Derry continued eyeing the table. "And I am sure the punishment is equally extreme. I'll pass on the anxiety, thank you. Besides, I have my hands full with other matters."

Nathan lined up his shot, knowing better than to pry into his business. If there was a serious issue afoot, the prince would tell him, eventually. He always did. The four of them knew far more about the inner, and incredibly dysfunctional, workings of the Warcian royal family than perhaps even members of the country's own court. The ball missed its target entirely, and Nathan muttered another curse.

"Troubled?" Derry asked. "You are usually a decent match for me."

"He's besotted with Miss Arabella Hughs, the wallflower assigned to him."

Nathan glared at Lockhart. "I am not besotted."

"And that's why you haven't been able to keep your eyes off her from the moment you knew of her existence, in spite of your spectacular failures to secure the waltz."

"She found out about the bet," he supplied to Derry. "So I've been on my best behavior in order to sway her to my cause."

"Is that really all?" Thurmont inquired. "I must agree with Lockhart. You've been mooning at her spectacularly since the beginning of the house party. Even Miss Caroline couldn't distract you."

"It does sound like things have gone well beyond this bet," Derry said, casually leaning down to make another perfect shot. "Will you court her?"

"Will she let him?" Kirkwood asked from behind his book.

Lockhart crossed his arms with a smirk. "Now that is the question of the hour, isn't it?"

"Are you still mad about me intervening during the bowling game?" Nathan said, hoping to divert the unhelpful conversation. He hardly knew where his own feelings lay, and his friends pontificating on the matter was not helping him sort things out in the least.

The response had the intended effect, as Lockhart's smirk fell into a frown. "I was merely perturbed at having lost the rare opportunity to cajole the impossible mark I've been given. I'm terrified to know what punishment you have in mind in the likely chance of my failure, Thurmont."

"You'll have to wait and see at the end of July," Thurmont replied with a gleeful grin. The man was taking far too much pleasure in Lockhart's suffering. Deciding to get some air and free himself from any further scrutiny, Nathan set down his cue with a nod to Derry. "I concede defeat. I think we both know the game is a lost cause."

Derry shrugged. "Very well."

"I think I might enjoy a walk," Nathan called to the others. Lockhart and Thurmont were arguing again, but the former gave him a distracted wave to signal that they wouldn't be coming along.

"The moon is full tonight," Kirkwood said, pulling the book from his face at last, if only for a moment. "The lake will be beautiful, as you well know."

"Thank you, Kirkwood," Nathan said as the marquess shoved his nose back into his reading after nodding. He turned to Derry. "And you?"

"I'm tired from the long journey, but thank you. You look like you need some time to yourself, regardless."

"Yes, I think I do." After a last farewell to his rowdy friends, Nathan made his way outside. Deciding to go along with Kirkwood's implicit suggestion, he walked through the gardens and made his way towards the lake path. The moon was indeed full, and the air crisp. He took a refreshing inhale of the summer grass scent as he walked, the soothing hum of crickets lulling him into relaxation. Andrew had enjoyed night walks, and Nathan often accompanied him as a child. The memories of his brother sneaking into the nursery, cakes hidden in his waistcoat whilst he cajoled Nathan to join him for stargazing, were some of his most precious. It was time taken well for granted by his foolish adolescent self. There was a flash in his mind of the last time they'd spoken, of the harsh, petulant words passed between them, and Nathan took another bracing inhale to keep the wave of dark sadness at bay.

He finally reached the large hill that hid the lake, so similar to the one on his own estate where he and Andrew had stared at the stars. He blinked at the figure standing atop it, and for a moment thought his brain had conjured the spectre of his dead brother. But no, the silhouette was feminine and familiar. He stopped in his tracks at Miss Hughs, her form illuminated by the moon and bracketed by the stars. The mere sight of her sent his despairing heart fluttering, and Nathan had no idea what to do about it.

CHAPTER NINE

NATHAN HAD STARTED the walk back for only about a minute before hearing the distinct sound of footsteps following him. He didn't stop despite the hurried pace with which he was being pursued.

"Milton, wait," Miss Hughs rasped behind him, her voice breathless from her trot.

Knowing it was futile to ignore her, he stopped and turned around. She wore only a pale walking dress that all but glowed in the silver moonlight. Her hair was uncovered, tendrils falling from her chignon as she took several deep breaths. He watched the rise and fall of her chest, momentarily transfixed by the creamy skin illuminated under the moon. "What is it?" His words came out harsher than intended.

She was close enough now that he could see the details of her face. Her brow scrunched. "I…"

"You?" he prompted, putting an impatient hand on his hip. Her reasons for following him were a mystery, and he almost resented the fact that she'd intruded on his walk and thrown him out of sorts with her glorious presence. Her current behavior was entirely at odds with what he'd assumed her feelings for him were, and he was growing impatient with his inability to know where they stood.

Miss Hughs squared her shoulders and cleared her throat. "I wish to discuss what happened the other day."

"You mean the kiss?"

There was a pause before she continued, her voice a tad more steady. "Yes. I've been trying to speak with you regarding the matter, but you seem determined to avoid me." She sounded irritated with him, which was perplexing.

"Is that not what you wanted?"

She huffed. "What I wanted was to work out whatever this—" She waved a hand between them. "—this *thing* is between us."

He flicked a brief glance back to the house. They were close enough that one might see their shadows in the moonlight, and considering the gaggle of ladies he'd nearly stumbled into a few minutes earlier, this spot on the path was not private. "This is not a good place to have such a conversation." Perhaps the course of action he was about to suggest would be a mistake, but Nathan could think of no other solution. "Follow me."

For a moment, he wondered if she would even do so, but after a few seconds of walking, he could hear her light steps trailing behind him without complaint. He made his way to the back of the house, being sure to stay hidden in the shadows once they got closer to the monstrous structure. It was a path Nathan was long familiar with, having taken part in many a forbidden late night outings with Thurmont and the others during their boyhood. Miss Hughs said nothing as they walked, only her stiff footsteps in gravel as they traversed the side of the house interrupting the silence. He almost wished she would speak, if only to break the awkward tension building between them. Finally, they reached the back gate to the gardens. He undid the latch and held it open with a flourish. "After you."

Miss Hughs paused on the threshold. "We really shouldn't meet like this."

"And yet, here we are," he replied. The time to return and come and gone. If she was going to give him the opportunity to talk, then he would seize the moment and not give her a chance to run from him again. "No one will come upon on us back here so late in the night," he assured. The dark, winding paths of Thurmont's purposefully wild garden would be unappealing for anyone who wasn't up to some secret business, making the chances of someone coming upon them unlikely. He hadn't seen any light in the house during their trek, and most others wanting a moonlit walk would likely choose the same path that the other ladies had. Nathan hoped for the frolicking women's sake that no else had come up with the same idea as he had done.

"I'm not sure if that is a good or a bad thing." She spoke playfully, but the implication hung in the air between them, forcing him to swallow a swift wave of warmth.

Inwardly berating himself to stay on task, Nathan followed her through the gate as she finally walked through it. "You needn't worry on that front," he said. "You made your disgust of me quite clear."

She stopped, so suddenly that he'd nearly slammed into her back, and whirled on him. "Why in the world would you think that?"

Once more, he couldn't help but to admire how the moonlight shone over her luminous skin, her paleness emphasizing those wide, mesmerizing brown eyes before the meaning of her words hit him. "You liked it."

"I didn't say that," she replied hotly. Though he couldn't see it in the dim light, somehow Nathan knew she was blushing.

"You implied it," he shot back, crossing his arms with a triumphant smile even as his mind reeled.

"It doesn't matter. This was a mistake." She turned away from him and made to walk away.

He grasped her wrist in a gentle grip. "I'd say it matters a great deal."

"Please," she said, not turning around. "Don't pretend some great attraction for me. My pride can take many things, but this is going a step too far."

"I pretend nothing." When she did not move, he stepped closer until her back nearly touched his chest.

She smelled like the lavender sprig he'd given her, and the thought of hauling her against him and taking in that fresh, summer scent was unbearably arousing. His want for her could no longer be denied, and he'd wondered when this need had gotten so out of hand. He thought back to the lake, when the morning sun shone over her like a halo and her delicate lips had curved in amusement at his antics. And then he saw her at the ball, slender neck craning to spy him across the room, brown eyes wide and curious. Had it really begun that early? Nathan wasn't sure, and didn't think it quite mattered at the moment. Right now, there was only one thing he wanted and one thing only, as much as his rational mind was screaming at him.

"You know what I think?" he asked softly, resisting the urge to rest his hands on her slight shoulders. He wondered if the skin of her collarbone was as soft as it looked.

"I don't care," she whispered but did not move from her spot.

"I think," he continued on, ignoring her response, "that you want me to kiss you again."

Miss Hughs turned around to face him once more, her mouth drawn in a thin, uncertain line as her eyes scanned his face. For what, he wasn't sure. "You are very sure of yourself," she muttered. And yet, despite the insult, she took a minuscule step forward.

"I'm never sure when it comes to you." He smiled, slow and seductive, raising a hand to stroke her cheek and waited for her to move away, or for some other sign his actions were unwanted. When she did neither, he lowered his head, all the while wondering just what was about to become of them.

———

Milton was going to kiss her again, Arabella realized with muted but warm surprise. She should stop him, should turn on her heel and walk away or lay a flat palm on his chest and give him a good hard shove. She did none of those things, too captivated by the angular planes of his face in the bright moonlight and the fuzzy heat spreading from her chest as he grew ever closer. She took a step forward, only half realizing it, and tilted her head at the same time he lowered his. He'd been entirely right. She did want him to kiss her, and that longing overpowered all rational thought until it was the only thing Arabella could think about.

Their lips met in a flurry of sensation, melding and separating in a soft, languid caress. His tongue swept along her bottom lip, teasing into the seam of her lips. The fission of heat in her chest slithered down her body to pool between her legs, and she parted her mouth with a quiet whimper. He in turn let out a low groan, hauling her against him, and Arabella could only wrap her arms around his large frame as he plundered her mouth. His hand grasped her buttom and, rather than the action shocking her, she was only emboldened further. Clutching the fabric of Milton's coat, Arabella pushed into him, tongue darting out to meet his. A hardness pressed against her belly, and she flushed with the knowledge of what it meant. Arabella had spent enough nights giggling over a smuggled lurid tome or two with Caroline to understand just what this embrace could lead to. For her to have such an effect on a man was positively thrilling.

A twig snapped somewhere deep in the garden, and the interruption was enough to jar her from the haze of arousal she'd been trapped in. Milton pushed away from her at the same time as she, both of them staring at each other in muted shock. They remained frozen and silent for a good minute, and Arabella strained her ears for any other sounds to indicate another's presence. Nothing happened, but that relieving fact didn't soothe her. "What in the world was that?" she spat harshly into the dark.

"Probably an animal," he replied with a shrug.

"That wasn't my question, and you know it." She wasn't sure what infuriated her more, the bewildering lapse in her judgment or the fact that he seemed completely unbothered by this devastating episode.

He put his hands on his hips, a undercurrent of irritation lining his voice. "What do what me to say, Miss Hughs? One second you seem to hate my very presence and the next you're letting me kiss you. Twice, might I add."

"I..." She swallowed, her mind a confused frenzy. Though the sound had likely been nothing, the reminder that they might have been discovered in such a passionate embrace did nothing to ease her disquiet.

Milton had tried to trick her, made himself a complete ass, and foisted his unwanted company on her at any opportunity. And yet, he was also charming, entertaining, and seemed to appreciate her in a way that no other had before.

Or did he?

The bet still hung in the air, and it was entirely possible that he was still playing at the ruse, that his affections were merely a more strategic way to win in the long run. The thought was enough to cool any remaining ardor, panic and embarrassment replacing the feeling with a force that nearly took her breath away. She'd sworn last year to never fall for another deception, to never play the moon-eyed fool for some duplicitous man.

"Miss Hughs." His voice was quiet, almost soothing, as he reached for her.

She took a step back with a shake of her head. Everything was still too fresh for her to process properly, his presence too distracting. Space between them was required, and fast, for the almost somber look in his eyes nearly drew her into his arms once more. Before her discipline could snap, Arabella turned on her heel and ran. This time, the lack of footsteps behind her was a relief.

———

"Is everything alright, Bella?" Caroline peered at her from her place on the sofa. They were lounging together in Arabella's room before breakfast. A ride was planned for the day, and everyone was up earlier than normal. "You've been acting strange all morning. Did your excursion last night not go well? I hope the ladies were not horrid after all."

"No," she replied, so quick and loud that Caroline visibly startled. Arabella took a staying breath before continuing in a more moderated voice. "It was... wonderful." Wonderful, confusing, and terrifying in equal measures.

"I'm glad you enjoyed yourself," Caroline said in relief.

"Yes, I did."

"I suppose it would be exquisite under the light of the full moon."

"Yes, he was."

There was a choke as Caroline nearly spit out her tea. "What?"

"What?" Arabella flushed, realizing her mistake.

"We're not talking about the lake, are we?" Her sister set her teacup down and frowned. She leaned forward, giving Arabella a probing look. "Spill."

Dodging the interrogation was futile. Arabella well knew how stubborn Caroline could be when she wanted something. "Fine," she grumbled, her face reddening. "I kissed someone."

Caroline gasped. "Milton kissed you?"

Arabella blinked. "How did you know it was Milton?"

Of all the reactions she'd expected her sister to

have, it certainly wasn't the frantic clapping and squealing currently happening. "I knew he liked you!" Caroline settled herself and grasped Arabella's hands, though she looked on the verge of another excited fit. "Tell me everything."

"You…" Arabella struggled for words, too shocked by this warm reception to her news. "You aren't upset with me?"

"Upset? Why on earth would you think that?"

"Our mother was pushing you two together, and you didn't seem to mind."

Caroline rolled her eyes. "Of course I'm going to be excited about spending time with a duke. That doesn't mean I want to marry the man."

Relief coursed through her at the revelation. If Caroline had indeed been interested in Milton, Arabella wasn't sure she would have been able to bear it. The guilt alone would have eaten her alive. "I'm glad."

"To be honest, I could tell you were mad for each other from the moment you met."

Arabella blinked and then laughed at the ludicrous assertion. "We are not mad for each other."

"Then what are you?"

Arabella paused. "I'm not certain."

"What do you mean 'not certain'?" She pointed an accusatory finger at her. "I've been plotting since the beginning of this blasted house party to shove you two together. Surely that must count for something."

Arabella stared at her sister as if she'd grown a second head. "I don't understand."

"Fist off, I've done nothing but gush about you to him whenever we conversed. It's just about all I talked about, and he seemed enthralled whenever the topic came up."

"He did?" That warm, fuzzy feeling built anew.

Caroline continued without acknowledging the reply. "I tried steering him to you at luncheon before you fled." She softened her gaze. "For perfectly understandable reason, of course. And then, I went to all the trouble of feigning an ankle injury to get out of bowling in the hopes that His Grace could gravitate to you instead without our mother breathing down his neck, but then Lord Lockhart went and ruined things." She threw her hands up. "Matchmaking is exhausting. I can't imagine how mother keeps up with it."

"Does she know about this little plan of yours?"

"Are you insane?" Caroline scoffed. "I'm already the Duchess of Milton in her eyes, and nothing will convince the woman otherwise, even if holding the title is just about the last thing I want. No offense to your Milton, but I don't think we have a single thing in common. When he isn't asking me questions about you, he's going on about horses. I barely know how to ride one adequately, let alone enthuse about them." Horsemanship was one of the few things Caroline never learned well, no matter how many instructors were employed for the task.

"He is not 'my' Milton," Arabella said.

"What is he if not yours? You've kissed the man twice now, might I remind you." When Arabella didn't reply, Caroline fell back on the cushions with a groan. "If you'd just acknowledge that you're perfect for one another, then we would all be in a far better place."

Arabella clutched her hands. "I don't know about that."

"Bella." Caroline sat up on her elbows, a soft, serious edge bleeding into her voice. "He is not Lindsay."

"No, he is not," she admitted. "Even with the bet."

"Bet?" Caroline straightened with a frown. "What bet?"

Arabella described the details of the wager she'd overheard. "I suspected he was only paying me mind in order to convince me to help him get that horse. But now, I am not so sure."

Caroline looked thoughtful. "He seemed far too interested in you for that to be the only factor. A man doesn't look at a woman like that over something so trivial."

"And you would know how?" Arabella said with amusement.

"When one gets the amount of attention that I do," Caroline explained matter-of -factly and without a hint of gloating in her voice, "you become very skilled at discerning who is genuine and who is false. Last year, I sensed Lord Lindsay's duplicity from a mile away."

"I should have listened to you back then," Arabella said. Her sister had warned her of Lindsay's false affections, but Arabella had been too happy to have someone prefer her over her sister for once in her life that the warnings had fallen on deaf ears, much to her embarrassment after the fact. She waited for melancholy to slither into her heart at the memory. Oddly, only a dull ache needled her heart, one that had far more to do with the burn of humiliation than any lingering feelings for her former and deceitful suitor.

"I don't know if I ever told you this, but I poured a cup of tea over his head when he proposed to me," Caroline said with a happy smirk.

"You did not tell me that, no," Arabella said with a small laugh. She could imagine the scene with vivid clarity, and the thought of the viscount sputtering as the hot liquid splashed into his meticulously quaffed hair was enough to chase the troublesome memories away. "Thank you."

"Milton is different, Arabella." Caroline crossed her arms. "He likes you. Do something about it."

But she was still unsure of herself, and unsure how to properly proceed. Perhaps Caroline was right and Milton's interest was genuine, having nothing to do with winning the bet and everything to do with his regard for her. But the stubborn fear that her sister was wrong, that her own budding feelings would be squashed once Milton realized his task was well and truly a lost cause, kept her frozen with indecision.

There was a knock on her door, their shared maid

sliding in a moment later. Happy to have a momentary diversion from her dilemma, Arabella rose. "We will have to continue this discussion later, for it is time to prepare for the ride."

"Oh, that? I'm not going," Caroline said with a cheeky smile. "Terrible headache, I'm afraid. Be sure to tell mother when you find her downstairs."

Now that she thought about it, Caroline only wore a simple walking dress rather than the required riding habit. "Mother will be displeased. No doubt she expects you and Milton to spend the ride together."

"Which is precisely the point." Caroline stood and walked to Arabella, giving her a playful pat on the head. "With me out of the way, you will be free to monopolize His Grace's time. Now then." She strode to the door with a cheerful spring in her step. "I'm off to languish in bed for the rest of the day." She opened the door and made to walk out, but poked her head around before shutting it. "If I don't hear half the guests gossiping about you and Milton at dinner, then I shall be very cross with you, sister."

"Get well soon," Arabella replied with a laugh as Caroline ducked back and shut the door with a definitive click. She feared her sister would indeed be quite cross, for Arabella had no clue how to move forward.

Chapter Ten

Nathan eyed Miss Hughs from across the room, balancing a barely picked at plate in his hands, and wondering what was on her mind. She stood with Lady Drummel, who kept sending irritated glances towards the door. Miss Caroline was notably absent, and he wondered if that had anything to do with the woman's agitated state. Miss Hughs looked at him for the briefest of moments, their eyes meeting, before turning away to listen to her mother.

His entire plan regarding her had been rocked on its axis with the revelation that their attraction was mutual. He'd acted a supreme rakehell last night, smothering and pawing at her like some untried schoolboy. Any other lady might have demanded a proposal right there, and yet she'd fled. He wasn't sure how to proceed. Did she desire a courtship? Or was there to be nothing more between them than a sudden, passing lust? The answer was unclear, and her refusal to even glance in his direction wasn't helping matters.

"And what do you think?"

Nathan turned to his mother, who sat beside him on a chaise. Breakfast was served buffet style in the drawing room, the long ride set to follow right after, though the duchess planned not to go. He gave her an apologetic smile. "I'm sorry, mother. I was woolgathering."

The duchess eyed him over the rim of her teacup. "I was suggesting that you might spend the ride with Miss Caroline. Felicity and I thought it a capital idea." She gave a pointed look to the corner he'd been gazing at, or rather, the person. "But I suspect that our attempts in that area are unwanted."

Nathan tried not to flush at his mother's keen observation. He should have known better than to hide anything from her. "Miss Caroline is lovely," he began, "but she isn't... isn't..."

"Her sister?" his mother replied with a knowing smile.

He failed to hide his blush this time and took a large bite of eggs with an exaggerated swallow. "I apologize for not saying anything," he murmured, so as not to have anyone overhear. "You seemed so enamored of Miss Caroline that I hesitated to disappoint you."

"Do not fret about such things," she replied with a gentle pat on his knee. "I merely thought she would be a good match. If it is the elder Miss Hughs that has caught your eye, then I am more than pleased to hear it."

"The thing is, mother," he replied, setting down his cutlery with a mild clank. "I'm not sure Ive caught *her* eye, and I don't think she is the type of lady to be swayed by my title."

She set her cup down. "Then show her your good qualities. Perhaps spend some time with her?"

He glanced in Miss Hugh's direction once more. Her back stayed stubbornly turned towards him as Lady Drummel prattled on. He wondered if what the woman had to say was truly interesting or if Miss Hughs was merely engrossed in the conversation so as to not have to turn around and see him again. Nathan suspected it was the latter. "I think I may have scared her off."

His mother frowned. "Whatever do you mean?"

"Nothing," he replied quickly, likely too quickly. "I only mean that I may have been a bit too forward in our last interaction. Considering her dislike of me, I'm sure any of my subtle intimations were confusing and unwanted." There was nothing subtle about kissing a lady twice, but he certainly would not share that much with his mother. Though the woman knew him so well that he wondered if she even believed the excuse he'd just given.

Likely not, if her deepening frown was any indication. But, rather than call him out in the middle of breakfast, the duchess shook her head with a wry smile. "Well, whatever you did, I'm sure it isn't as bad as you think." She lowered her voice even more. "Surely it cannot be worse than Miss Russel's attempts to get Thurmont in her court. The poor girl seems besotted with him, and I am reasonably certain he wants nothing to do with her." She cast a meaningful gaze behind him.

Subtly, so as not to be seen staring, Nathan followed her direction. Indeed, Miss Russel was as glued to Thurmont's side as she could be without seeming improper and appeared to be talking his ear off. No doubt she planned to maneuver herself to spend the ride by his side. Thurmont looked about ready to jump through the nearest window. He winced as Miss Russel laughed at something she'd said, the sound grating enough to draw the attention of the rest of the room. Mrs. Parsons was nowhere to be seen, and Nathan wondered where she might be, for her poor charge was making quite the fool of herself. He turned back to his mother with a grimace. "I suppose you are right."

His mother nodded. "I am." She gave him another encouraging pat. "Why don't you try to spend the ride with Miss Hughs? I know you usually enjoy galloping ahead with His Highness during these things, but this may be a splendid opportunity to talk to her."

"I believe I shall," he said, having already decided on such before their conversation. Whilst they certainly wouldn't be able to discuss the matter of their relationship so openly, he could at least make himself available as charming company and perhaps lighten the air between the two of them. One thing was for certain, however. If he was to make any progress with Miss Hughs, he would have to tell her he'd already given up on the bet. Whether she believed him was another story entirely, but Nathan would cross that bridge when he came to it.

The butler came and announced that the horses were ready. With a brief kiss on his mother's cheek, Nathan rose. His eyes never left Miss Hughs as she followed the group, but before he could maneuver himself closer, a hand on his arm stayed him in the hall. He turned to see Thurmont, who gave him a pleading look. Nathan rose an eyebrow as the rest of the group shuffled out, leaving them alone in the hall. "Are you quite alright?"

"My God, man, you must help me." Thurmont flicked a quick, panicked glance to the door before looking back at him. "I fear she plans to follow me around for the rest of the day."

Amused by his friend's silly distress, Nathan gave him a soothing smile. "Miss Russel? For a moment, I thought something was actually wrong. Don't scare me like that."

Thurmont shook his head. "I wouldn't expect you to understand, what with you mooning after Miss Hughs."

"There's that word again. I am not 'mooning'." Mostly.

But Thurmont ignored the reply. "You must help me. Derry was supposed to be here for me to hide behind, but he wandered off to god knows where, and Kirkwood is hiding in the damn library again."

"And Lockhart?" The baron had been sulking in the corner of the parlor for the entirety of breakfast, glaring daggers at Miss Balfour as she spoke to a young gentleman whose gentry family neighbored Thurmont and had been invited to the ride.

"He's determined to succeed with Miss Balfour and declared he could be of no aid, being busy with his own scheme to follow the lady around for the day."

Nathan sighed. "So you want me to take your attention during the ride and prevent any openings for Miss Russel to sidle up beside you?"

Thurmont smiled and nodded. "Precisely."

The earl truly had no one to turn to, and if Miss Russel genuinely made the man so uncomfortable as to resort to such methods, then Nathan would be a terrible friend to leave him to his suffering. That did, of course, mean that he wouldn't be able to spend time with Miss Hughs. "Dammit, fine," he said with an exasperated grumble. "But be prepared for hard riding. We can leave Miss Russel behind." And Miss Hughs, much to his disappointment.

Thurmont gave him a hearty clap on the arm, his tense shoulders easing. "I'll repay for the favor, Milton. Thank you, truly."

"You better," he grumbled back, his plans for Miss Hughs entirely in disarray. He could only hope the woman didn't think he was avoiding her on purpose.

———

"Well, isn't this just perfect?" Arabella grumbled as another rumble of thunder rolled across the cloudy sky. She peered around the mossy forest, hoping that one of the myriad trails branching off from hers would be familiar. The ride had been fast-paced, and Arabella had strayed well behind the group for most of the day. At one point, she'd stopped to admire the scenery, which had been a colossal mistake, as by the time she was finished, the group had gotten far enough away that she'd been unable to discern where they'd gone. Thinking that they'd perhaps rode into the forest, Arabella had chosen one trail and hoped for the best. She should have turned around long after realizing how lost they were, but, stupidly, she'd assumed that the path would double back, eventually.

'Assumptions are dangerous things, child.' Lord Drummel's words echoed in her ears, one of the few times her father had deigned to pay her any mind. Far preferring his clubs over his wife and daughters, she rarely saw him outside of breakfast, wherein he hid behind a newspaper in a silent order to ignore his presence. As much as their relationship had strained over the years, Arabella still pitied her mother for being stuck with such a disinterested spouse, one who'd almost completely ignored her once it became apparent no sons would come about.

A droplet of rain struck her nose, and Arabella cursed aloud. "Aren't you supposed to know the way home?" she grumbled to her horse, an old doddering mare suited to her lackluster riding capabilities. The mount lowered her head to munch on some grass in response, and Arabella gave her an affectionate pat on the neck with an exasperated sigh. She would need to hurry before the inevitable downpour began. No doubt it would take a while for anyone to realize she was missing. She had been relegated to the back after all, and Caroline wasn't in attendance. Still, the thought that not a single rider in the party had noted her absence stung. Of course nobody would, she reminded herself. Cecily had been downright accosted by Lord Lockhart, whilst Mrs. Parson had been busy minding Miss Russel, whom seemed determined to spend the entire afternoon mooning after Lord Thurmont to an almost embarrassing degree. The earl and Milton had galloped on even farther ahead of the already speedy group, making her wonder if it had been a ploy to avoid poor Miss Russel. It was entirely reasonable that she might be overlooked. And yet, no matter how many rational explanations her brain conjured up, the mild burn of tears persisted with the knowledge that she was well and truly on her own and unimportant enough for no one to take notice.

"Calm, Arabella. You are being ridiculous." Self pity would get her nowhere. Best to focus on the warm cup of tea and quiet sketching that awaited her once she found a way out of the forest. As if fate itself were mocking her, the small drops that had begun sprinkling the forest grew heavier and more frequent until the skies opened up to let loose a horrid downpour. She jumped with a shriek as a clap of lightning slammed into a nearby tree, bathing the area in a violent flash of white. Before she could even get her wits about her, the horse reared up with a startled cry and Arabella went tumbling to the ground. She took a bracing gulp of air as her back smacked into the dirt, but had thankfully missed the jagged rocks peppering the little-used trail. She laid there a moment to catch her breath, listening to the distant sounds of her mare's thundering hooves as the beast fled. "What am I even doing here?" she mused quietly to herself, closing her eyes as a stray tear mingled amongst the rain.

Despite the icy water pelting her face and the mud seeping into her clothes, it was an oddly peaceful moment. It was just her, sprawled in the soft mud, and the tranquil patter of rain against the leaves. For a moment, she forgot everything; her lackluster seasons, the disdain of the Ton, even whatever disaster was brewing with Milton. Was it her, or was her brain conjuring up his voice? She could almost swear to hear his lilting tenor through the fog of her mind.

"Oh, my dear Milton," she said with a giggling sigh.

"Yes, it's me, darling. Can you open your eyes?" The voice pierced the fog, warm hands cupping her cheeks as she obeyed the request. Milton's face came into view, eyes were wide with terror and mouth pursed as he surveyed her person. His hair stuck to his face most becomingly, she thought nonsensically before reality hit.

"Wait, you are actually here?" She glanced about, but winced at a piercing ache in her skull. The forest was dim, the afternoon light fading into dusk. "I was unconscious," she realized. Perhaps her head had hit a rock after all.

"I thought you were dead when I found you sprawled on the ground. You were so still."

"You were looking for me?" She peered up at his relieved face, the heat of his palms seeping into her cheeks. It made her realize how cold she was, and she shivered.

"I've been searching this forest for the past two hours."

"You were looking for me from the beginning?" She said faintly, warmth bubbling in her chest. "I didn't think anyone noticed I was missing."

"Of course I'd notice. I'm aware of you at all times, Arabella." A feeling emerged within her, something aching, something familiar, something that terrified her to no end. Another crack of thunder sounded before she could respond, though it was likely only one of many that had sounded off in the time she'd been unconscious. What a miracle to have slept through such a tempest.

"We need to get you out of here before you freeze to death." He removed his palms, much to her dismay, and cradled her head in one hand. "Can you sit up?"

"I think so," she said with a wince. She pushed

herself up with her palms, focusing on the task in order to forget the tempestuous feelings his presence was stirring within her.

He shrugged off his coat. "It's nearly soaked through but better than nothing."

She relished what little warmth was left in the garment as it was draped over her shoulders and pulled it around herself, taking in the scent of him along the collar despite how soaked it was. "You really were searching for me for this long?" Her voiced sounded meek.

"Indeed, I was. Several of us noticed you were gone and I, naturally, volunteered to find you, thinking you must have taken a wrong turn at some point. If I had known the severity of the situation, I would have brought more help." He looked down the trail, empty save for his mount loitering on the edge. "Though after how long it's been since I set off, a search party has likely been sent out by now."

"They noticed," she mumbled to herself, a small smile forming on her lips.

"Of course they did, you idiot. You're not nearly as invisible as you think you are." Before she could respond to the warming words, Milton put a hand to her back. "Let's get you up on Highwind. I'd rather not have you wait in this cold for the search party."

"Wait a moment," she blustered as his arm slipped under her knees. Before another protest could leave her lips, he'd stood with her in his arms. She felt the heat of his chest through his waistcoat and laid a flat palm on his chest to steady herself as he walked towards the horse. His heart hammered wildly beneath her fingers despite the business like air he donned, the pace of it likely mirroring her own. "I can walk," she protested shyly.

"I don't mind," he replied, his voice a ragged timbre. She was almost disappointed when the short walk to Highwind was at an end and he set her down. Perhaps she was imagining things, but it had felt like his hands had lingered on her person longer than was proper. "Can you mount him on your own?" he asked.

"I think so." She managed to haul herself halfway, but stumbled before she could sit properly. Milton grasped her waist in time and guided her to the proper place. The shock of his fingers brushing her hips was enough to make her more lucid. She exhaled as his hands released her until one palm rested on her knee. She looked down at him, cheeks burning.

His face was a blank mask as he stared at her skirts, and she watched, transfixed, as a raindrop slid from his soaked hair and down the sculpted planes. Milton looked up, eyes serious and solemn. "Miss Hughs... Arabella."

The sound of her given name coming from his lips for the first time all but stopped her heart. "Yes?"

"I gave up on the bet."

She swallowed. Here was the moment where he would admit his falsehoods and inform her that their time together was at an end. A tiny spark of hope ignited in her breast when his serious gaze did not waver, and she tried in vain to suppress it. "Oh?" Her voice was a pathetic whisper, barely surpassing the rain.

"I wish to court you."

That tiny spark exploded into a wave of happiness... and trepidation. A part of her wanted to leap into the fray and accept him, but another wished to take Highwind's reins and gallop away as if the devil himself were at her heels. "I..." She shut her mouth, heart and mind at war with each other.

"You do not have to answer me right away," he said when she didn't continue. "I know I've sprung this up at the worst of times. If you..." He looked away from her for the first time since beginning and frowned. "If you do not share my feelings, then I understand."

"It's not that," she protested. "I just... it's hard to trust again."

"I did start this whole thing on the wrong foot," he replied with a self-deprecating smile.

Arabella shook her head. "It is not the bet, not entirely, at least." She was going to have to tell him, she realized with a terrified jolt. He would need to know the tale of Lindsay in all its embarrassing entirety to truly understand her recalcitrance. "May I share something?" Her voice was timid as her brain screamed at her to stay silent. Surely he'd think her the greatest fool in the world were she to talk.

"You can share anything," he replied with an encouraging smile, in spite of the fact that, for all he knew, she was about to reject him spectacularly. It gave her the courage to continue.

"Very well," she replied, trying not to shake from nerves. "Let us make our way to the house as we speak."

"You read my mind." He gave her a playful pat on her knee, one that sent a pool of heat through her. She clung to the warmth and braced herself for the inevitable.

CHAPTER ELEVEN

NATHAN LED Highwind along the rocky paths, waiting for Arabella to speak. She was clutching Highwind's mane in a white-knuckled grip and staring at the forest ahead with steely resolve. He wouldn't push her, despite his burning curiosity. Finally, after another few minutes of silence punctuated only by the patter of rainfall and the horse's hooves, she spoke. "Do you know of a Lord Lindsay?"

"Not personally, but he frequents my club. He seems a shallow dandy, and others have a low opinion of him." Nathan remembered Miss Caroline's words when they'd been seated together at dinner. "Your sister told me he courted you last season."

Perhaps the observation had been a bit too forward, for Arabella grimaced. "My only courtship, in fact."

"I inferred that from the way she spoke of it," he replied. Now, Miss Caroline's panic at dinner after mentioning Lord Lindsay made a bit more sense. Things must have gone poorly, far more poorly than a mere mutual agreement of unsuitability, as was common with most other courtships.

"You must think it pathetic that I've had so little prospects," she said, tensing as if braced for some sort of insult.

But Nathan refused to humor her poor self-esteem. "I really do not care how many or how little suitors you've had. I'm interested in you because I like you. Simple as that." And it really was, now that he allowed himself to truly think about his feelings. His interest had started from the beginning and, looking back, it was rather silly that he hadn't set out to court her at the outset. "I hope you believe me now when I say that the damn horse had nothing to do with it, fine as she is."

"I'll have to meet her before the end of the party," Arabella replied, finally looking at him with a wobbly smile. If it were possible, Nathan would have kissed her, if only to turn that hesitant quirk of her lips into a full grin. The rain had slowed to a sedate drizzle, so he was at least able to make eye contact with her without having to blink the icy water from his eyes.

"I'll be sure to do so." He gave her leg another gentle pat of encouragement, knowing that she'd only mentioned the horse to stall whatever tale she was about to tell. "You were saying?"

"Right, Lord Lindsay." She let out a hard, long exhale before squaring her shoulders and looking just a tad more secure after their tangent. "My first season was mediocre at best. I received a handful of calls, but nothing more. The Ton just didn't take a shine to me, much to my mother's frustration. She placed all her hopes on my sister after that. Once Caroline had her come-out the next year, well, we all know how my prospects turned out." She absently stroked Highwind's neck, looking ahead once more. "I didn't resent Caroline for her success, genuinely, but..."

"It was still frustrating?" he supplied for her.

"Yes. I never took it out on Caroline, however, no matter what anyone thinks. She remained unengaged by her own choice, though I still am not sure why. There have been many proposals."

"Perhaps she merely wanted to wait for the right person?" That had certainly been his philosophy going into the wife hunt. Though, he thought as he watched Arabella's pretty face struggle to continue, he may not need to wait as long as Miss Caroline. "It is a smart way of going about things."

"I was not nearly so wise," she replied. "Not back then, at least. When Lord Lindsay began to approach me at balls, procuring a dance nearly every time, you cannot imagine my excitement."

"I'm sure," he replied.

"He made several calls, and for once I wasn't left alone in the drawing room corner whilst Caroline managed her insurmountable wall of gentleman."

"Insurmountable?" The image of the poor girl

managing a veritable hoard of silly suitors nearly made him laugh aloud.

She nodded. "Oh yes. With so many of them, it was nearly impossible for anyone man to claim her attention unless he could keep her interest to a reasonable degree, which was difficult. Though many assume it because of her beauty, my sister is not a frivolous person and requires stimulating conversation."

"Yes, I noticed that." Though they had had nothing in common, Miss Caroline had been an intelligent conversation partner, one who hadn't dithered in petty niceties about gossip or the weather. He was beginning to understand why the lady was so picky and, perhaps, where this unfortunate tale was going.

"He danced with me at every ball and even took me out on a few drives. There was one picnic we both attended, and we spent a good while walking about together."

Nathan remembered luncheon the other day and her stricken look as she spied him and Miss Caroline strolling through the garden. Perhaps the reminder had been what had set her off so egregiously, rather than their confrontation at the lake. "He was not actually courting you, was he?"

"No, he was not. I should have sensed something was amiss when he kept asking me questions about Caroline. At the time I had thought that he was merely trying to engage me in conversation, blind fool that I was. But no, he was merely trying to get an edge on his competition. 'Who would ever be interested in you,

Miss Hughs' was what he said to me after I'd pressed for more." Arabella looked positively mortified as she spoke, and it infuriated him to no end.

"What an absolute ass. Why did he not think that you would tell your sister of his duplicity?"

She shrugged. "I assume he thought the rumors of our bitter rivalry to be true." She shook her head with a small smile. "Ironic, considering that Caroline was the one to warn me about him in the first place. She has a knack for people, you see. Far better than myself."

"You couldn't have known. I would have thought the same thing were I in your shoes, anyone would have."

"But I didn't and got my heart broken in the process. It wasn't all bad, though. After I told her about it, Caroline led him along like a puppy dog for the rest of the season and brutally rejected his proposal. She poured an entire cup of tea on his head."

"Good," he replied, satisfaction thrumming through him at the vengeance. "And he was entirely incorrect in his assumptions. 'Who would ever be interested in you?'" He repeated Lindsay's question with a dramatic scoff. "An entire duke, that's who."

"Milton..."

He stopped walking and stared into his uncertain face. Even in the quickly fading light of dusk, he could see her eyes shining. "I know you are unsure," he said gently, "and I understand why. Just, please believe me when I say that you are the only woman I've ever met who has even come close to stirring my heart."

She took one plump lip into her mouth. Blast the current predicament they were in , for he wanted nothing more than to back her into the nearest tree and kiss her senseless. As if to emphasize that they were, in fact, in a very precarious situation, the skies took that moment to open up once more and a torrential downpour even worse than earlier fell upon them with raging fury. "Oh dear," Arabella muttered, hugging his coat tighter to herself.

The darkening sky roiled with thunder once more, a heavy gale sweeping through and whipping around his soaked clothes. They had yet to exit the forest, and even he wasn't certain they could find their way in the darkness were they not able to make it out by the fast approaching night. There was only one thing to do, as dangerous as the action might be to her reputation. "Arabella," he called over the rain.

"We need to find shelter," she replied.

"Yes," he said with a grimace. "I know."

————

Arabella watched Milton lead Highwind along with trepidation. "Do you know where you're going?"

He steered them down another trail, one going in the opposite direction than they'd been heading. "There is an old gamekeeper's cabin a little down the way. We liked to use it for a bit of a hideaway when we were boys. It won't be much, but we'll be sheltered until the storm passes."

"Can we not still make it to the house?" Surely he understood the precariousness of taking shelter together, alone and overnight. If knowledge of this were discovered, her reputation would be in shambles, if it wasn't already.

But Milton merely shook his head. "No," he called over the rain. "You strayed well off course, and I'm afraid the house is still a good few miles away. It would be far too dangerous in such a storm." As if to punctuate the statement, another bolt of thunder struck, close enough that the crackling boom made her jump in the saddle. Highwind, thankfully, was far more disciplined than her mare and merely took a few uneasy sidesteps.

"We cannot be alone like this," she declared.

"We're going to have to be. With any luck, Thurmont and the others will be the ones to find us once the weather settles. We could say that you found the cabin on your own, and I spent the night in the wilds searching for you. If Derry is kind enough to humor us and believe the excuse, then the rest of the guests at the house won't stir up a fuss, probably."

"Probably?" She repeated doubtfully.

"We either try that or announce our engagement," Milton replied. She saw his shoulders shrug in the gloom. "There's no choice either way, so let us get moving."

There was nothing she could say to convince him otherwise, and deep down Arabella knew he was right. She could only hope that events played out as he predicted and the men cooperated, else she'd be a duchess by season's end. Though, would that not be the same result were she to accept his courtship? Regardless, Arabella wanted space to decide if Nathan's feelings were true without the pressure of outsiders.

They meandered along the beaten path; the storm getting worse by the minute. Nathan was a silent silhouette in the rapidly fading daylight, and she could only trust his sense of direction and the surefootedness of his horse to get them to their destination safely. Just when the last bit of light was slipping from the sky, they emerged into a clearing with a small cabin positioned in its middle. "Here we are," Nathan called in relief, his voice hoarse from the exertion of leading Highwind along the rugged path. "Thank God."

"I worried we might never find it," she shouted over the roar of the downpour.

"For a minute there, I did as well." He led them to the door and helped her down. "Go ahead inside while I get him settled. If we're lucky, there will be some firewood inside for us to warm up with."

Trying not to become bothered by the reminder that they would be spending an undetermined amount of time alone together, Arabella went inside. It was dim inside, with nothing but a stone fireplace and dusty wooden floor to greet her. It was a sparse space, one that obviously hadn't been used in some time, but it was dry and protected from the elements, with no drips to be heard. Even better, she quickly located a small pile of firewood nestled along the wall. She made to move towards it, but swayed with a sudden dizziness. A pair of hands steadied her.

"Careful," Milton said against her ear.

Arabella realized just how alone they were in that moment and how long it might be before anyone came looking for them. Last night's kiss was fresh on her mind, the feel of his soft mouth and the pleasant tingle of arousal that had flooded her body after he'd hauled her against him coming forth with a vengeance. His chest had been so sturdy against her palms, the same chest that was now flush against her back.

"Shall we build a fire?" she blurted and took a step away from his heat, as inviting as it was.

"There is no 'we' involved." Milton moved over to the pile of wood and began sorting through it. "I will make the fire. *You* will sit your lovely self on the floor in front of it."

Despite wanting to protest, the weakness in her limbs only served to prove Milton correct. Slowly, so as not to stumble in an ignoble heap on the ground, she lowered to the ground and wrapped her arms around her legs in a vain attempt to keep warm. Resting her chin on her knees, she watched Milton mill about the fireplace. He was focused on his task, not speaking save for the occasional muted curse as he tried and failed to get a spark going, and she took the opportunity to consider the events of the previous few hours.

Telling him about Lindsay had been one of the most embarrassing moments of her life. Of all the reactions she'd been expecting, his uncompromising support of her plight and condemnation of her former suitor had not been one of them. For the first time in a long while, if ever, she felt like it was okay to lay the blame entirely on Lindsay, to acknowledge that she hadn't merely been too stupid to see the obvious signs. To have someone other than Caroline believe in her for once, to see the person beyond the pathetic wallflower she'd become, was a wonderful feeling and made Arabella want to believe in the man before her to an almost painful degree.

"Milton," she said, her voice barely a wisp of sound over the relentless pounding of the rain against the roof.

"Ha!" he shouted triumphantly as the spark took hold, obviously not hearing her muted call. "I knew I remembered from when we were boys."

"Milton," she tried again, a tad louder.

He only continued tending the budding flame and not turning around. "I'll have us nice and toasty in no time. If only we had some blankets."

She suppressed a smile, even as exasperation filled her. "Your Grace!"

"Hey now," he replied, turning his head with a frown. "I thought we were long past addressing me as such in private."

"You've been ignoring me, and I have something important to say."

The fire was now going steady, warmth emanating from the flames and spreading into the dark cabin. It was a welcome relief to her wet clad self. It was fully dark outside by now, and she watched the firelight dance across his handsome face as he smiled at her and stood. "You may share whatever you wish. Before that, however, you should get some of those soaking clothes off."

"Right," she realized, and slid his coat from her shoulders to unbutton her riding habit. She peeled the soaked garment off her arms and allowed it to fall to the floor. Whilst the cotton dress beneath was damp, the heat of the fire was able to pierce it enough to warm her skin. Milton plopped down next to her, still fully clothed. Arabella frowned. "Will you not at least remove your waistcoat? Surely you must be freezing."

"I do not wish to make you uncomfortable," he replied. "I'm sure this situation we are in is already enough for you."

She drew her knees to her chest once more and shyly peered at him. "I don't mind."

"Very well. Thank you." Milton hesitated for only a moment before untying the intricate knot of his cravat and pulling the garment off. His waistcoat followed, and she did her best not to stare at the hard planes of his chest revealed by the damp shirt as he leaned back on his hands with a content sigh. "That is much better, even if our clothes are still wet." He tilted his head towards her, blue eyes glittering in the firelight as his smile turned mischievous. "You *are* bothered."

Arabella snapped her gaze to the floor, a hot blush that had nothing to do with the fire staining her cheeks. "Any lady would be frazzled to see her suitor in such a state of undress."

There was the smallest of inhales before he replied. "Does that mean my courtship is welcome, then?"

She continued staring at the crackling flames, too shy to look at him. "Yes."

There was a shuffle before she felt a warm body sidle up against her. "Arabella," Milton murmured. He stroked a finger along her cheek in a gentle prompt to face him. His gentle gaze warmed her far more than any flame ever could. He grasped one her hands in his elegant fingers and kissed her knuckles. "I'll do my best not to muck things up. I seem to have a knack for that when it comes to you."

She laughed, even as her heart pounded. "I believe in you, Milton."

"Nathan, please. I think we've moved beyond titles."

She tightened her fingers around his. "Nathan." The name was foreign but pleasant to say, and this new intimacy sent a flutter to her stomach that rivaled any interaction they'd had before.

"May I kiss you?" he mumbled, his head inching closer.

"Please," she replied and leaned up to meet him. Their lips met with a silken caress, that familiar ache beginning to build as their mouths slanted together. His tongue leisurely teased her lips, and she opened to meet him in a gentle clash. After a few minutes, he pulled away, and she made her disappointment clear with a frown and a small hum of disapproval.

"Easy now," he replied with a mild chuckle. "I'll not take liberties whilst you are still injured. Besides," he wrapped an arm around her, his voice tickling the shell of her ear, "If we keep going I'm not sure I'll be able to stop."

His shocking words only made the ache worse, and she swallowed to suppress the lurid imaginings that her mind was conjuring. "You are right, I suppose."

"I'm always right," he said with playful arrogance.

"You and I both know that is untrue," she replied, though her words held no bite. She huddled into his side, enjoying the warmth of his palm as he stroked her arm and feeling more content than she had in quite a long time.

Nathan kissed the crown of her head. "When it comes to you? Absolutely."

Chapter Twelve

As Nathan had hoped, it was Thurmont who'd waylaid them as they left the cabin come morning. He was in the process of helping Arabella back onto High-wind when his friend emerged from the trees, Derry and his two guards flanking him. "We had a feeling you'd be holed up here, Milton," Thurmont called, pulling his horse to a stop before them. "And you found Miss Hughs."

"Safe and sound,I hope," Derry said, the mild smirk quirking his lips telling Milton that he had an inkling of what transpired.

"Very well, Your Highness," Arabella said as she settled on Highwind. She adjusted her skirts and looked the prince straight in the eyes. "I found this cabin last night and sheltered until morning. Milton only found me a few minutes ago." Her demeanor didn't change, even as Derry eyed her speculatively.

After a moment, the prince nodded. "I see. How

fortuitous. I'm sure your family will be relieved to know that you spent the night in relative safety."

"Everyone was in quite a state once we realized you were missing, Miss Hughs. And when Milton left the party to find you and still hadn't returned by sundown, the house was in a near state of pandemonium. Your sister, in particular, was quite distressed," Thurmont said. He looked at Nathan, a teasing gleam in his eyes. "And it looks like you've survived the night's cold well enough."

The tension within him eased with the confirmation that both men were going along with Arabella's near laughable excuse. No one at the house would dare question either their host or a prince, not openly, at least. In the event that their courtship didn't amount to anything, Arabella's reputation was safe, and they wouldn't be forced to the altar. The thought of another stolen rendezvous in the next week was enough to send a delightful shiver of anticipation through him. "Shall we get going?" he said to distract himself from his growing arousal.

As he'd predicted last night, the trek back to the mansion took nearly an hour due to the slow pace with which they needed to travel. Nathan felt Arabella's eyes on him for nearly the entire journey, and he tried his best to focus on leading Highwind through the rocky paths rather than stare back at her like the besotted fool he feared he was fast becoming. Thurmont and Derry were blessedly silent, but the knowing smiles the two shared when they thought he wasn't looking told him they were well aware that his relationship with Arabella had taken a turn for the romantic. He tried to feel embarrassed, but there was only a stubborn sense of contentment with him, as if he'd finally solved a great puzzle and achieved some great victory. Ironic, considering that he'd lost any hope of winning Bellona.

Miss Caroline was already halfway down the terrace steps when they finally approached the house, Lady Thurmont following with a handful of servants armed with blankets. His mother stood on the threshold, a hand on her chest. Even from the distance, he could see how pale she was. Hell, he thought with a cold pang; he hadn't even thought of how his impetuous rescue mission and temporary disappearance might have affected her.

"The duchess put up a calm and collected front the entire time you were gone," Derry said quietly after dismounting. "But she seemed immensely distressed."

"Milton," Arabella's soft voice took his attention. She smiled kindly. "Go to Her Grace. I will be fine from here."

He hesitated for only a moment, before Miss Caroline descended upon them in a tearful hurricane. "Oh, Bella!" she cried as Thurmont helped her sister from Highwind. She crushed Arabella into an embrace. "I'm so glad you are safe."

Arabella rested her head on Miss Caroline's shoulder. "I am alright. Do not fret." She looked at Nathan and nodded.

"We will talk later," he assured and, after ensuring

that Arabella was indeed taken care of, headed towards his mother. She'd already gone inside and was standing alone against a far wall. He put a hand on her shoulder. "Oh, mother. Forgive me."

She shook her head. "Please, do not apologize."

Nathan ignored the request and enveloped her in an embrace. She felt small and frail in his arms. "I wasn't thinking. I should have realized how gallivanting after Arabella in the middle of a storm might affect you. I should have—"

"Milton," she interrupted sternly and took one gentle step out of his arms. Her hands bracketed his face in a gentle grip. "Nathan. I am alright. You scared me, yes, but going after Miss Hughs was the right thing to do. I've come a long way these past ten years, and have had much time to come to terms with my grief. I wanted to take this season to finally move forward with my life, so please, do not treat me as a fragile child."

He swallowed at the words, knowing in his heart that they were true. He'd spent so much time trying to carefully consider his mother's feelings, that he hadn't taken a moment to question how much she wanted him to. "I'm sorry, mother."

"There you go apologizing again. I told you to stop, did I not?" she commanded, ever the brilliant duchess.

"Yes, m'am," he replied, straightening his back.

She shook her head with an amused chuckle before sobering. "You've managed to build a life for yourself beyond Andrew and your father, and for that I couldn't be more proud. Now, let me follow your example."

Nathan could only nod, his throat tightening.

She rubbed his shoulder. "Now then, do tell me why it's 'Arabella', now and not Miss Hughs."

A flush overcame him as he realized his mistake. "We... had time to talk after I found her."

His mother raised an eyebrow, grinning like a cat cornering a mouse. "And was that last night or this morning? I know about that gamekeeper's cabin that you always liked to spend time at as a boy whenever you visited Thurmont." The grin snapped into a frown. "Milton, tell me you did not spend the night with her?"

He felt his blush turned ten shades darker. "Not like that." Mostly. "We merely sheltered together from the storm."

"I see." The look he received in response told him that the woman didn't believe the answer for a second.

"Everything was most proper," he lied. "But please, do not say anything. I've gotten Arabella to agree to a courtship, and I do not want to force her hand with the threat of ruination."

The duchess's eyes lit up. "A courtship, you say?" She smiled triumphantly. "Looks like my first intuition was right after all."

"Whatever are you talking about?" he asked with a curious smile.

"To be frank, when I first met Felicity's daughters,

it had been the elder Miss Hughs who'd first caught my eye and who I thought might interest you. But then, of course, that mess happened at the end of the night, and I shifted to Miss Caroline. I'm now entirely convinced that the exchange was all your fault. Oh, this is so wonderful," she continued at a rapid pace. "When are you proposing?"

"We aren't that far along yet, mother," he protested lightly.

"Yet," she repeated. The color had fully returned to her face by now, and he feared she was about to vibrate with excitement.

"Remember, please go along with the tale Thurmont and Derry gives everyone."

"Yes, yes. That is indeed the wise course of action. Not that I would have said anything, anyway. Oh, I am so happy you found your duchess so quick."

"We shall see." He wouldn't set himself up for disappointment and would keep his expectations reasonable. He sensed that Arabella still didn't trust him completely, and if that wasn't addressed soon, everything would come crumbling down around them.

———

"Sketching my handsome face, I hope?"

"You wish," Arabella said with a small laugh as she continued working on the drawing. She surveyed the glimmering lake before bowing her head over the drawing once more. It had been nearly a week since that disastrous ride, and the house party was almost at an end. She'd recovered from her ordeal within a day, much to the relief of Caroline and even her mother, and was able to participate in the remainder of the party. Normally, she would have relished the excuse to stay holed up in her rooms and away from company. Now, however, things were different. Much different.

She smiled as a pair of arms wrapped around her waist, pulling her against a warm chest. Nathan rested his head on her shoulder. "A penny for your thoughts, my dear?"

"Just thinking about this past week", Arabella replied and continued to sketch in the cage of his arms. Nathan had danced attendance on her at just about every activity, making his intentions more than obvious to everyone else. Caroline had been delighted at the news of the courtship, while her mother had given tight lipped approval. Perhaps the woman was upset that Caroline hadn't been chosen, or was embarrassed that the child she'd put no faith in was potentially about to secure the match of the season, but Arabella didn't let the lukewarm reaction bother her. She was far too happy to care.

Nathan was kind, charming, and a wonderful companion. There was a calmness to their courtship, a serene relaxation that was nothing like her awkward, shallow exchanges with Lindsay. Nathan didn't pile her with meaningless complements, nor fill the silence with inane chatter, but rather proved himself to be a steadfast companion, whose easy conversation and quiet admiration had her eagerly looking forward to every new day with him.

She was half in love already.

"It's been a marvelous week," he said. "Though I must state a preference for these dawn meetings of ours."

"I agree." Every morning she went to the lake to sketch, and every morning Nathan would conveniently cross paths with her on his morning ride. They'd spend the remainder of the morning lounging by the lake, with him laying on the hill as he watched her draw and, on occasion, crawling over to give her a clandestine kiss or two. Arabella could envision them having this routine forever, and a larger and larger part of her was hoping it would be so.

"Do you have a lake on your estate?" Her heartbeat quickened after asking the question. It was the closest she'd come to a direct acknowledgment of their potential union. Whilst they'd agreed on a courtship in the cabin, Nathan hadn't brought up the topic for the rest of the week. She appreciated the lack of pressure on his part, but the longer she didn't have a confirmation, the more her irrational anxieties gained traction. Perhaps she should ask him plainly if he planned to propose, but such a direct action brought on an entirely different host of nerves.

"Not as spectacular as this," he replied, not taking the admittedly vague hint. "But the countryside is quite beautiful, and we have a wonderful spot to look at the stars. Andrew took me there often as a boy."

There was a wistful sadness in his voice at the mention of the deceased man, and Arabella knew that now wasn't the time to bring up her worries. "You've never spoken of him in detail to me, or the late duke." He was silent, and she worried the question had been too presumptuous. "You do not have to tell me about them if I am prying."

"You weren't prying." He disengaged from her and sat down to her left. "I just wasn't sure where to start at first, but it is something I would like to share with you." He stared out into the lake before continuing. "I cared for my father, but we didn't get on well. Andrew had been such a staid, well-behaved boy growing up that when my difficult self came along, he didn't quite know what to do with me. I wasn't even an expected child, as mother had struggled to conceive in the ten years after my older brother's birth. Where Andrew had been easy, studious, and eager to take on his responsibilities, I was a bit of a hellion, being set back from school several times and chafing under the expectations placed upon me."

"He didn't understand you," she noted. Her own father hadn't even made the attempt, but Arabella wondered if he would even like her were the dour man to try.

"The duke loved me in his own way," Nathan mused. "He just didn't know what to do with me and kept his distance. Andrew, however, was different." He looked away from her again, and she could see the tightening of his throat.

"We don't have to continue."

"No. I'm alright," he persisted. "Andrew doted on me from the moment I was born. My mother joked that he was in the nursery more often that she was. Most of my childhood memories are of him trundling around the estate with me on his shoulders." He smiled to himself, as if reliving the memory. "To be honest, he felt more like my father than the duke himself, but that proved to be a double- edged sword. He chastised me often when my school troubles began, and I chafed under his attempts to bring me to heel once I grew old enough to get into more adult trouble. It was out of love for me, I know this now, but I didn't appreciate it at the time." Nathan looked down into the grass, his voice lowering. "We had a bitter argument the last I spoke to him, and I left in a rage, declaring I'd never speak to him again. Their carriage overturned that night."

"Oh, Nathan. I'm so sorry." She understood now why he'd been so sensitive to her rumored bad relationship with her sister. Arabella couldn't imagine losing Caroline under such circumstances. Just the very thought was enough to burn her eyes. When he didn't respond, she sidled closer and leaned against him. "Thank you for sharing that with me."

"They would have liked you, both of them. Though," he quirked his lips as he looked down at her. "You would have had to be content with a second son." The words carried with it a certain implication, but Arabella knew this was an inappropriate time to ask for clarification. Instead, she merely nestled further into his side. "You could be the tenth son of a mister, and I would still be sitting on this bank with you."

"Arabella..." He gazed at her for a moment before leaning down for a kiss. Though her worries still persisted in the back of her mind, Arabella could only focus on the gentle spring breeze and the feeling of Nathan's soft lips gliding over her own.

Chapter Thirteen

NATHAN STRODE into the billiards room, trying his best not to smile like a lovesick fool for the amusement of his friends. Thankfully, only Thurmont and Lockhart were inside, Derry and Kirkwood likely having wondered off as they were wont to do after dinner.

"Someone is happy," Thurmont noted with a smirk as Nathan shut the door. It seemed that he went so good at hiding himself after all.

"At least someone is having a good time," Lockhart grumbled, once again clutching a decanter of whiskey as he sulked on the sofa.

"Oh, don't mind him," Thurmont said. "He's just sulking because Miss Balfour has been spending time with Mr. Lambert."

Nathan rose an amused eyebrow as the baron only scowled harder. "The neighboring gentleman? If didn't know any better, Lockhart, I'd say you were jealous." It had been a mere jest to ribald the man, but

Lockhart didn't take the bait, only frowning into his glass as he took a long swallow of whiskey. Concern replaced Nathan's earlier mirth. "Is everything alright?"

Lockhart waved his hand. "Don't mind me. Just upset that I'll be losing that bet is all."

Nathan knew his best friend well enough to realize that there was more to it than that, but now was not the time to confront him on the matter. "Well, I'm sure you gave it your best shot."

"You still have two months," Thurmont chimed in. "Miracles happen. Speaking of miracles," he tuned his attention to Nathan. "I see that you've had just the opposite luck from our hapless friend here."

"That is putting it lightly," he replied, his mood swelling even more at the thought of Arabella. "I am reasonably confident that I have found my duchess." More than reasonably, if he were being obvious. The last week with Arabella had been sheer bliss, every moment spent with her proving more glorious than the last. Her dry humor and intelligent conversation charmed him, and she seemed genuinely engaged when he spoke of his passion for horse breeding. Her own excitement as she spoke of her love for painting was infectious, despite himself never having picked up a brush or pencil in his life. He could imagine her now, perched somewhere on his massive estate and drawing the rising sun as he came to join her after his morning ride, much like their clandestine meetings at Thurmont's lake.

The memory of this morning was still fresh on his mind. Arabella was the only other person besides Lockhart that he'd told the full details of his last moments with Andrew, and the fact that he'd had no qualms with sharing such a raw, visceral part of his past had solidified his decision. Arabella was to be his duchess. There was no other woman he could even begin to imagine filling that role besides her.

"Fallen in love with your mark, eh?" Thurmont teased.

Nathan blinked and considered the words before realization hit him. "Actually, I think I have." The revelation wasn't shocking and merely caused a bubble of warmth to settle in his chest. The feeling was only natural, considering everything they'd been through. Whether she returned the sentiment, however, was another thing entirely. Arabella liked him, that much was obvious, but he was unsure if her feelings went beyond that.

Thurmont looked at him as if he were some strange specimen. "Congratulations, I guess. I cannot say I envy you placing your heart in the hands of someone who could easily crush it, but to each his own, I suppose."

"Don't damper his good news," Lockhart said as he rose from the sofa. He clapped a hand on Nathan's shoulder. "I'm happy for you, even if I cannot fathom it myself."

"Don't be so quick to doubt," Nathan replied. "I

fear you might find yourself unprepared if the time comes for you to feel this way."

"Ha!" Thurmont interjected with a laugh. "Lockhart is even more of a hopeless case than myself when it comes to love, and that is really saying something."

"Your loss," Nathan said with a shrug. "Both of you."

"Hardly," Lockhart snorted. "But thank you for the sentiment."

"I suppose I'll be losing dear Bellona," Thurmont said with a mournful sigh.

It was on the tip of Nathan's tongue to correct the assertion, but something kept him from saying so. These two weeks had been such a wonderful experience, and he was loath to put a damper on things with something as vulgar as whatever punishment Thurmont would conjure up. He supposed he could ask Arabella to dance a waltz at some point during the season, but it was the principle of the matter. He wanted to assure her that he was serious about giving up that offensive wager, and leave no room for her to doubt his intentions. At the same time, he'd rather delay his inevitable humiliation. Perhaps he could let Arabella know he was only pretending to go along with things to delay the inevitable. His impending doom could be a source of amusement for the both of them.

All that in mind, Nathan leaned against the billiards table with a casual grin. "You suppose correct. I'll ask her for a waltz at tomorrow night's ball." It was the last event of the house party, the lavish affair drawing in the surrounding aristocracy and even upper gentry to pad out the numbers. It would be the perfect place to cement his victory, not that he was going to be dancing in the first place. He'd come up with some reason to fail, but his friends need not know that. Perhaps he and Arabella could slip out for a clandestine moonlit stroll instead.

"You can take Bellona with you when you leave, if you wish it. I see no way that you could fail now."

Nathan looked at Lockhart, preparing to tease him about attempting a waltz with Miss Balfour, only to see the baron paling at the sight of something just behind him. "I think there is one way, Milton," he murmured urgently and jerked his chin. Nathan turned around and froze at the sight of Arabella in the doorway. She must have been eavesdropping, for he was almost certain that he'd closed the door.

Her pale face was stony, her mouth set in a grim line. "I see."

"How much did you hear?" he said and winced at the inadvertently incriminating question.

"'I'll ask for the waltz at tomorrow night's ball'," she repeated, her tone one of cruel mockery.

"We'll just see ourselves out," Lockhart said, awkwardly backing from the room and pulling a cringing Thurmont along with him. Arabella allowed them to pass, her icy gaze never wavering from his person as the door quietly closed behind her.

He tried his best not to panic. "Will you let me explain?"

She crossed her arms. "I doubt anything you say will fix things." Her face twisted as she cast her gaze to the floor. "I cannot believe this is happening to me again."

"It's not. Please, listen to me." He reached her in three long strides and grasped her hands. "I'm not going through with the bet. I just didn't want to tell them yet in order to stall for time. Thurmont plans to have me do something humiliating, and I wanted to wait a while. I was going to tell you, I swear it. Arabella, look at me." He swallowed at the sight of her tear-stained cheeks, and knew what needed to be said. "I love you."

"How dare you," she hissed and wrenched her hands from his grasp.

His heart sank. "You don't believe me."

"I'll never believe you, not after what I've heard." She shook her head. "Everything makes sense now."

Irritation replaced his anxiety. "Does it? Or is that what your low self-esteem is telling you? I want to marry you Arabella, but if you cannot trust me, then there is no way forward for us." His tone was harsh, borne more out of hurt and frustration, and her stricken face told him he was going about this the entire wrong way.

"Then we are done here," she replied before squaring her shoulders with a loud, sniffling inhale through her nose. "Good evening, Your Grace." She wrenched open the door and stormed out. He winced as the door slammed shut, his heart sinking to his toes. He ran a hand through his hair, wondering what to do next, if there was even anything to be done. Whilst he'd phrased things poorly, he'd meant his earlier words. If there was no trust between them, if he had to spend his life with her questioning his every action, then there really was no future for them. Pain bloomed within at the thought. He was beginning to understand why Lockhart and Thurmont seemed determined to avoid love, and Nathan had the distinct feeling that Arabella was about to crush his heart in her hands as he'd been warned.

———

Arabella realized she might have made a colossal mistake once morning came and she'd told Caroline of what had transpired yesterday evening and the words exchanged between them.

"You called it off?" her sister said incredulously, sitting at the foot of Arabella's bed.

Arabella sat up straighter and tucked her knees to her chest with a hearty sniffle. She'd spent the night and most of the morning alternating between crying and doubting herself, and had even skipped breakfast lest she see Nathan's face again and crumple once more. "I didn't know what else to do after what I'd heard."

"Half a conversation?" Caroline sighed and

scooted closer, resting a hand on her knee. "Arabella, why did you not believe his explanation? It makes sense that he didn't want to cast a pall over the courtship with the consequences of that stupid bet. And he said he loves you."

She buried her head into her knees, the doubt that had tormented her all evening coming back. "I'm scared of trusting him."

"Do you truly not believe him?" Caroline continued gently, "Or is it that you do not believe anyone would feel so strongly about you?"

Nathan had suggested the same thing, though had stated it far more harshly, perhaps out of hurt more than anything. Arabella clutched the fabric of her nightgown as tears threatened once more. After overhearing his muffled conversation with Lord Thurmont, she'd immediately decided to cast him aside, to put him in the same box as Lord Lindsay without a second thought despite his proclamations.

'I wish to marry you, Arabella.'

She thought on the words, and the emotion with which he spoke them. Would he really have gone as far as a marriage proposal for a mere wager? Shared the painful story of his deceased family? The answer was obvious and made her want to curl up in bed and cry all over again. "I've made a colossal mistake."

"I think we've already established that," Caroline replied dryly. "The real question is what you plan to do about it."

Arabella lifted her head and wiped a stray tear

from the corner of her eye. "Where do I even begin? I must have delivered quite the blow."

Caroline nodded. "You should have seen him at breakfast. The man looked positively morose, so much so that I didn't dare approach him."

The observation only confirmed her mistake, and a sharp stab of guilt pierced her chest. "Will he even speak to me, I wonder?"

"Oh, don't be so melodramatic," Caroline replied with a roll of her eyes. "Of course he will. He loves you, and you love him, correct?"

"I do," she admitted. Far longer than she'd realized, in fact. Arabella wasn't sure when her irritation and exasperation with his antics had turned into fondness, but it was perhaps earlier than even she cared to admit. Right now, however, what mattered was salvaging that love before it was too late. "How should I proceed?"

"That's the spirit," Caroline said cheerfully. She put a thoughtful finger to her chin. "I think you should show that you trust him completely, that you are willing to move on from your past and believe in others."

It was a tall order, and Arabella struggled to come up with an action that would convey such feelings to their fullest extent. "The house party ends tonight, and I fear he may leave me completely if things remain as they are. He may not even return to London, for all I know." The thought of him fleeing to the countryside for an indefinite amount of time, letting the fragile thing they'd built whither away because of her impulsive actions, made her grow cold.

"I think I have an idea," Caroline said.

Hope stirred. "Oh?"

"Dance with him."

———

Arabella loitered in the foyer, peering at the stairs every few minutes and fighting the growing panic every time she didn't see Nathan coming down them. It was well into the evening by now, the ball in full swing, with nearly every neighboring family crammed into the expansive ballroom. In between watching her sister manage the veritable hoard of gentlemen angling for a dance and conversing with Cecily, whom seemed determined to remain on the edge of the dance floor, Arabella had waited with bated breath for Nathan to appear. Yet, as the evening wore on with no sign of him, anxiety had set in. She'd excused herself some minutes ago, hoping to catch him when he came down, but was now loitering around like a fool in the silent hall.

"Where are you, Nathan?" she muttered to herself and absently adjusted one of the sapphire combs in her hair. She and Caroline had taken great pains to dress her to perfection, even their mother allowing Arabella to wear jewels normally reserved for Caroline. The prospect of snagging the duke had softened the woman to her somewhat, and though Arabella knew it had more to do with the prestige she was about to bring to the family rather than any maternal affection, she would take any help she could get. Now, however, it seemed all their efforts might be for naught.

Another few minutes went by in silence, with no sign of anyone at the top of the stairs. Arabella shifted from one foot to another, impatience mingling with fear. It was becoming more than apparent that Nathan would not attend the event, leaving her entire plan in shambles. Something had to be done, and soon, lest the night wind down and they miss the last waltz of the evening entirely. Deciding to act before she could talk herself out of it, Arabella strode across the hall. Taking one look around her to ensure nobody was watching, she trotted up the stairs.

If Nathan wasn't going to come to her, then she would go to him. It was risky to disappear from such a large event, but perhaps her near invisibility would serve her well for once. Besides, if all went as planned, there was a good chance she'd be betrothed by tomorrow. It was a bold conclusion to draw, she knew, but such optimism was the only thing keeping her from turning on her heel and running back down the stairs. Trying her best to remember which door she'd seen him coming in and out of during the past two weeks, Arabella continued walking down the corridor before stopping in front of the room she hoped was his. She slowly pressed her ear against the door. Encouraged by the muted shuffling she heard within, Arabella stood back and rapped on the door. She held her breath when it opened to reveal Nathan's handsome form behind it. As she'd feared, he was still dressed in his day clothes. He looked her up and down with wide eyes.

"Um, hello," she said, shy and tongue-tied at the sight of him. Every word she'd rehearsed for this moment fled as nerves took over.

"You..." He blinked before shaking his head. "What are you doing here?"

She swallowed and cleared her throat, trying to organize her thoughts into something coherent. "I've been waiting for you all night." She stared at the knot of his cravat and clenched her skirts. "We have a waltz to dance, after all." When a moment passed in silence, his silent form unmoving, her nerves and sinking heart got the better of her. Heat stained her cheeks. "I'll go." She made to turn around, before his hand shot out to grasp her wrist.

"Wait," he said.

She tilted her head to look at him, hope blooming in her chest. "May I come inside?"

He visibly swallowed. "Is that wise?"

"I hope so," she replied.

"Very well." Nathan looked left and right down the hall before ushering her in and closing the door behind them.

Gathering her thoughts and knowing that her next words would be crucial, Arabella smoothed her skirts. "I wanted to apologize for yesterday." She inwardly cringed at the stilted statement.

"It is alright. I understand." He clasped his hands behind his back.

"No," she shook her head. "You were right that my lack of trust had more to do with myself than what I'd overheard. Deep down, I believed your explanation. If my stupid insecurities hadn't gotten in the way, I would have... I would have happily accepted your proposal. If that was even a proposal in truth. You didn't ask me directly, and I do not want to presume anything or—" She interrupted herself with a deep breath, realizing that she was beginning to ramble. After a long exhale, she continued. "I love you, Nathan, and I want to move forward in my life with you by my side. I thought, perhaps, that giving you that waltz would prove my trust, show that I know you won't abandon me once the bet is secure. So," she held out her hand, everything riding on this moment, "will you come downstairs with me?"

"No."

Her heart sank, and she looked at the floor, unable to face him. "I see."

Soft footsteps sounded until he was mere inches before her. His hand reached out and gently nudged her chin. "Look at me." Blinking back tears, she did as he bade and froze at the brilliant smile on his face. "I do not want to dance with you, darling, not right now. The gift you offer is wonderful, but I'll still not go through with Thurmont's bet. All I wanted to hear was that you love me as ardently as I do you. So, to answer your question." He cupped her face in his palms and leaned down to rest his forehead against hers. "Yes, that was a proposal, bungled as it was, one that I hope you have an answer to."

Arabella let out a wobbly laugh, heart soaring. "How can it be anything but a yes." She playfully tapped his chest with her palm. "You cad. I had this whole thing planned out with my grand gesture. You would have been swept off your feet, and we'd waltz at midnight. Caroline assured me it would be terribly romantic."

He huffed in amusement. "You'd have hated everyone staring and you know it. Besides, I've already been swept off my feet just by looking at you. You're stunning tonight, and I thought my heart was going to stop when I saw you at the door." He stroked a finger along her necklace. "The sapphires suit you. When we're married, I'll buy you your own set." The finger lingered on her chest, stroking the soft skin of her collarbone.

She shivered at the contact. "I don't want to go back down."

"Don't say such tempting things."

"I'll say whatever I want," she replied with a grin. Feeling brave, Arabella leaned up and kissed him. All thoughts of the ball fled as their lips met, the light touch of their mouths quickly devolving in a fiery clash of tongues as the kiss deepened. She pressed against him with a low moan and wrapped her arms around his waist.

He pulled away and gazed at her with half-lidded

eyes. "If we don't stop now and head downstairs, I'm liable to make love to you."

The words did nothing but fan the flames of her ardor, and she pressed against him more fully. "I told you, I don't want to go back down."

"The lady has spoken," he replied with a half grin. "Who am I to deny her?" He gave her another searing kiss that sent her toes curling before trailing his mouth down her neck. She tilted her head to give him more access, the slick slide of his tongue against her pulse sending a bolt of pure lust down her body. "Turn around," he whispered into her neck. Heart pounding, she followed the command, pulling her gloves off whilst his deft fingers worked their way down the lacings of her dress. The garment slid from her shoulders and pooled at her feet, followed by her stays before she could even blink. His hands paused in the process of bunching her shift. "Is this still alright?"

"Yes, please," she whispered, the anticipation almost too much to bear, and lifted her arms as he hauled the fabric off her. She shivered as the cool air hit her bare skin, relishing in Nathan's warmth as he pulled her against him.

He kissed the side of her head, hands skimming along her naked body. "Your so lovely." His hands cupped her breasts, and she leaned back against him as his thumbs gently ran over her taught nipples, thighs pressing together against the pleasant ache between her legs. He nibbled on her earlobe. "Don't close them."

Breath quickening at the request, she parted her

legs as his hand slid downwards. She bit her lip with a small whimper as he teased her slick folds, fingers sliding over her swollen nub and sending jolts of sharp heat into her. She squirmed her hips against his ministrations, moaning as he stroked her more brusquely. "Oh, God, Nathan."

He wrapped his other arm around her waist in reply, holding her in place as his fingers continued sliding roughly over her center. "Yes, my love, come on my hand."

Her head fell back as a delicious pressure built to an almost intolerable level. A sudden white hot pulse exploded with her center, and Nathan's mouth covered hers as she cried out from the force of it. His hand massaged her through the final waves of release, wringing every last pinprick of pleasure before slipping from between her legs and gently stroking her hip. Arabella tuned around in his arms, resting her head against his chest as her body calmed into a haze of satisfaction. His erection pressed into her abdomen, and the reminder of his own arousal stirred her once more. "Its hardly fair that I am the only one undressed, don't you think?" she said, looking up at him.

His eyes were hazy with lust, mouth quirking with a lazy grin. He rubbed her cheek. "Get in bed, and I'll join you shortly."

"Alright," she said, grasping his arm to kiss the side of his wrist. "But don't take too long."

"Aren't you forward?" he replied, and began undoing his cravat.

Arabella herself wasn't sure where this bravado of hers was coming from, but she preferred it over crumpling in a shy, embarrassed heap as her mind was screaming at her to do. Before those nerves could win out, she sauntered over to the bed and sat on the edge. Every sound of his shuffling clothes reverberated in her ears, and she busied herself with removing her stockings to keep her pounding heart in check. After scooting backwards to lie on the bed, Arabella sat up on her elbows and braved a look at her betrothed as he tossed the rest of his clothes off and stood proudly before her. Her gaze trailed from his handsome face, down a well-muscled chest, and lean hips. She glanced away from his jutting manhood with a heavy blush.

"Do I please you?" he teased with an arrogant smirk.

She flopped on her back with a giggle, the loose combs shifting in her hair. "Is that even a question?"

"I certainly hope not," he replied, his voice lowering to a sultry baritone. His footsteps padded across the room, and she held her breath as the bed sunk with his weight. She held out her arms and spread her legs as he approached and settled himself in her embrace. Nathan kissed her temple, cheek, and finally her lips, tangling his tongue leisurely with hers and moving his hand between them to gently rub her sex once more. She sighed into his mouth as the ache returned, before gripping the counterpane as the fingers were replaced by the head of his manhood. He pulled his head back, bracing one arm next to her head and pushing into her. Arabella clutched his shoulders, wincing at the mild burn as he filled her completely.

"Wrap your legs around me," he said, his eyes never leaving her face as she did so. After a moment, the discomfort subsided, and she felt only a slick, delicious friction as he moved within her. She rolled her hips to meet him with a low moan, tightening her thighs around his hips in a silent plea to continue. He buried his head into her neck, moving in a steady, firm rhythm that had her gasping and panting into his shoulder as the pleasure built anew, his own moans in her ear only bringing her closer to the brink. She came with a warm, pulsing throb, running frantic fingers through his hair and letting a breathless cry. He followed her with a low groan, burying his face into her neck and stilling. His weight fell atop her, and she basked in the cozy warmth of his body flush against hers. After a few minutes, he rolled away, and Arabella snuggled up to him, splaying a possessive hand over his bare chest as his arm wrapped around her waist. "That was better than dancing."

He huffed out a breathless laugh and kissed the crown of her head. "It tends to be, yes." His other hand reached out and began gently pulling the combs from her hair.

"It's a disaster, isn't it?" Arabella mused.

"Well, you aren't going back downstairs, that's for sure."

She made herself more comfortable against his side. "That's fine by me. For all they know, I've pled a headache and spent the rest of the night holed up in my room."

He rose an eyebrow. "Will they really believe that?"

She shrugged. "The headache? No. But avoiding balls is expected of a prickly wallflower like me."

"You are not a prickly wallflower," he replied sternly. "Not anymore."

Arabella looked up at Nathan's face, chest fluttering at the open love in his gaze. "No," she replied with a small smile. "I suppose not."

About the Author

Nicole Bennett is a writer of historical romance from Baltimore, Maryland. When not crafting tales of dashing rogues and charming debutantes for your reading pleasure, she spends her time prowling museums with a wonderful husband in tow and caring for two rambunctious feathered companions.

To learn more and join the mailing list, please visit: https://www.nicolebennettbooks.com

Other Books By This Author

Infamous Ladies

Chasing Scandal

Seeking Ruin

Courting Seduction

Waltzes and Wagers

The Duke and The Debutante

The Baron and The Bluestocking

Manufactured by Amazon.ca
Acheson, AB